# NIGHTMARES!
## HOW WILL YOURS END?

### VALLEY OF THE
### SCREAMING STATUES

By Don Wulffson

An RGA Book

PRICE STERN SLOAN
Los Angeles

ISBN 0-8431-3863-7
First Edition
10 9 8 7 6 5 4 3 2 1

**Library of Congress Cataloging-in-Publication Data**

Wulffson, Don L.
    Valley of the screaming statues / by Don Wulffson.
        p. cm. — (Nightmares! How will yours end?)
    "An RGA book."
    Summary: The reader chooses the outcome of a teenage boy's nightmare in which he searches a Malaysian jungle for his missing brother and anthropologist father.
    ISBN 0-8431-3863-7
    1. Plot-your-own stories. [1. Nightmares—Fiction.  2. Malaysia—Fiction.  3. Jungles—Fiction.  4. Plot-your-own stories.]
    I. Title.  II. Series: Wulffson, Don L. Nightmares! How will yours end?
PZ7.W9626Val 1994
[Fic]—dc20                                                          94-22679
                                                                             CIP
                                                                             AC

COVER AND INTERIOR ICON ILLUSTRATIONS BY DOMINICK DOMINGO.

*For Barbara Schoichet, the gifted, hard-working, and wonderfully tenacious editor of this book.*

—D. W.

# How to Find Out How Your Nightmare Will End

**T**ry to stay awake—you won't want to miss any one of the exciting endings in *Valley of the Screaming Statues*. Most of them are nightmarish . . . but if you're lucky, you'll pick the right route and find your way back to reality. Will you choose to confront the natives who hiss like snakes, or will you take the mysterious trail that has suddenly appeared before you? Should you follow the advice of Leander—even if he does have four legs—or try to walk through the wall of rain that now blocks your path? The choice is yours, and here's how it works.

First turn to the next page and learn where your nightmare takes place. Read on and find out which friends will be joining you. Then your adventure begins in a quest to find your long lost father and brother in the Valley of the Screaming Statues.

It's easy, it's fun, and it's very, very scary. Just read to the end of each section and follow the directions. You will be offered a choice of pages to turn to, or else instructed to simply go to the next page. And what happens when you reach the ending of one story? Why, just go back, make a different decision, and take a whole new frightening route!

Ready to begin? Good luck . . . and **Sweet Dreams!**

# THE SETTING

You are sleeping over at your best friend Chris Muñoz's house. You, Chris, and his little sister, Darlene, are all watching television. Chris is sprawled out on the sofa, Darlene is in the easy chair, and you are lying on top of a sleeping bag. The show you are watching is set in a jungle, and it reminds you of your missing father and brother. You don't want to watch, so you close your eyes. Slowly you feel yourself falling asleep. You let yourself drift off—but you wouldn't have if you had known you would end up in a horrible nightmare.

Your nightmare is set deep in a Malaysian jungle. Chris and Darlene are tramping through the brush with you as you search for your missing father and brother. The heat is horrible. It saps your strength, but you and your friends plod on. There are gorges and mountains, swamps and flatlands, raging rivers and foul-smelling lakes. More often than not, you are plunging into dense, damp foliage. Stinging insects make you miserable, and spiders, snakes, and other creatures lurk everywhere. Ever so often you come across a village. Sometimes the natives are friendly. Sometimes they are not.

In this dream-world setting, the jungle can suddenly change, mutating in shape and form.

Unexpected things may happen to you and your friends when you come across certain people, places, and creatures. Yet this jungle is not like any other, for it holds within its depths the Valley of the Screaming Statues, and therefore it is highly unstable, strange, and totally unpredictable.

## CAST OF CHARACTERS

**CHRIS MUÑOZ,** 14, is tall and gangly. He has long, curly hair and blue eyes magnified by thick glasses. He's a talker and has a dark, quirky sense of humor. Most people think of him as intelligent but rather odd and eccentric. He is your best friend.

**DARLENE MUÑOZ,** 12, is Chris's little sister. With her long, dark hair and impish grin, she is cute and lots of fun. But sometimes she's a bit of a pest. She annoys Chris, who teases her a lot.

**YOUR FATHER,** a professor of anthropology, has been missing since you were seven. His last letter, which arrived from Malaysia, said that he was going into the jungle in search of the Valley of the Screaming Statues. No one has heard from him since.

**YOUR BROTHER, DOUG,** now 21, was 19 when you last saw him. He ran off to Malaysia to find your father and, like him, never returned.

**YOUR MOTHER,** also an anthropologist, was going to go to Malaysia, too, until letters from your father warned her not to come. Now because he and your brother never returned, she is overprotective and will hardly let you out of her sight.

**W**hen you were seven, your dad went on an expedition to the jungles of Malaysia to find what the natives of the region called the Valley of the Screaming Statues. He and his expeditionary group never returned. Nor have any of the others who went looking for them, including your own brother, Doug. It has now been nearly two years since you've seen Doug and over seven years since you've seen your dad. With their disappearance, you and your mom have become very close. She always wants you around. It is as though she is afraid to let you out of her sight, afraid that you will also disappear. It is a monumental event to get her to let you do anything . . . until tonight. Finally, your mom has agreed to let you sleep over at your best friend Chris Muñoz's house.

With his long hair and thick glasses that magnify his eyes, some people avoid Chris. They think he is sort of scary looking, and his weird sense of humor sometimes puts people off. But Chris is your best buddy. He's super intelligent and a real crack-up. He's always babbling away, saying outrageous, funny, wacky things.

Now, in your well-worn jeans, T-shirt, and sneakers, you are lying on top of your sleeping bag, and Chris is curled up on the couch. You are both

*Turn to the next page.*

watching TV in Chris's living room when in walks his little sister, Darlene. She's cute and bubbly, but she can be a pest sometimes.

"Mind if I join you?" asks Darlene, popping open a can of soda.

Chris groans and looks over his shoulder. "Go home," he says.

"I *am* home," answers Darlene, plopping down in an easy chair. "I live here, remember?"

"Go live somewhere else," says Chris, pulling a blanket over his head.

You laugh at the exchange, then grow sad. You and your brother got along great and used to joke around in pretty much the same way. You try to focus on the TV. A movie that takes place in a jungle is on. You don't want to watch and you're tired. Why fight it? Your eyelids droop. You feel yourself drifting off to sleep. And then you fall. . . .

You're in a hot, insect-infested jungle full of animals. You know that you're dreaming—but *are* you? The dream seems so real. You want to wake up, to be back in the safety of your friend's living room, but you can't.

"This way," says a familiar voice.

You turn around and see Chris emerging from the jungle. Darlene is close on his heels.

*Turn to the next page.*

"Where are we?" Darlene asks you.

"The jungles of Malaysia," you explain.

"How do you know we're in Malaysia?"

"My dad sent postcards," you answer. "We must be here to look for the Valley of the Screaming Statues."

Chris wipes sweat from his brow. His glasses are all fogged up. "Isn't that where your dad and brother vanished?"

"Yeah, and I'm going to find them."

Darlene looks worried. "But which way do we go?" she asks.

You study the terrain. A broad, black-green river flows by below. A few yards ahead there is a trail that leads inland, through the jungle.

*If you take the inland route,*
*turn to the **next page**.*

*If you take the river route,*
*turn to **page 17**.*

You have decided to take the inland route. At first the going is easy. The trail is wide. But gradually the going gets tougher. The trail becomes steep, then it narrows. It is clogged with vegetation. You, Chris, and Darlene are stroked and scratched by creepers and brambles on every inch of your bodies. Underfoot is a soggy, springy carpet of rotting leaves and mud. The heat is stifling, and with the humidity, it is like being in a steam bath.

Just when you feel you are about to pass out, you come to a fork in the trail. One heads east, one heads west.

*If you choose the trail going east,*
*turn to the next page.*

*If you choose the trail going west,*
*turn to page 48.*

Headed east, you find the trees are flesh-colored, and crawling over them are countless numbers of giant slugs. Their bodies bloating and turning red, they appear to be sucking blood right from the trees! As if that isn't repulsive enough, minuscule monkeys with tiny human heads crawl over the huge slugs, feeding off of them as the slugs in turn feed off of the trees.

You are disgusted, and Darlene looks like she's going to be sick.

"Let's head back and take the river route," she says. "It has to be better than this."

Quirky Chris has a whole different take on things. He is transfixed by the weirdness of it all. "I love freaky stuff," he says, actually picking up one of the monkeys.

"You're sick!" Darlene squeals.

Chris just laughs at her. "Yeah, and that's one of my better qualities."

Chris and Darlene start to bicker. She wants to head back. He wants to keep going.

Finally Chris turns to you. "I want to see what other weird things we can find," he says, "but it's your dream. What do *you* want to do?"

*If you decide to keep going,*
*turn to the next page.*

*If you decide to turn back for the*
*river route, turn to* **page 17.**

As you continue, the eastward trail levels off, and you find yourself moving along a plateau. A small mountaintop village comes into view. Excited at your approach, the villagers hurry forward to greet you.

"We are looking for the Valley of the Screaming Statues," you explain to the people.

Their eyes immediately fill with fear. They become very restless, talking rapidly among themselves and waving their arms in frantic excitement. They don't calm down until their chief, an old man whose face is a brown webwork of wrinkles, steps forward.

"It is there," says the chief, pointing off toward a rocky jungle below. "But do not go. It is a place of evil, of magic. If you go, you will not return."

Chris puts a hand on your shoulder. "I think this dude is giving us good advice. I mean, like, I'm not in the mood for curses and stuff like that."

"But maybe my brother and dad are there."

"Sorry, pal, but I'm not going another step."

"Me neither," says Darlene.

It is clear that their minds are made up. But how about you? Are you too afraid to go into the Valley of the Screaming Statues alone?

*If you head off alone toward where the chief points, turn to the next page.*

*If you choose to head back with your friends, turn to page 38.*

Now that you are alone, this nightmare jungle is doubly terrifying. It takes all your will power to keep going. Telling yourself that you can handle anything, you head down into the dark gorge, picking your way carefully in the shroudlike mist.

Suddenly you hear a soft whispering coming from somewhere ahead in the eerie, foggy gorge. It sounds like human voices, voices calling to *you*, and you alone. *"Come,"* they whisper. *"Come!"*

The mist swirls. You catch a glimpse of what appear to be statues. Again the mist closes, obscuring the world ahead from view. You are frightened. You want to turn back. But you can't. Your feet keep moving you forward, deeper into the gorge. It seems you are under a spell, under the control of some unearthly force. Your pace begins to slacken. You are getting strangely tired. Your feet feel heavy, weighted down. Your thinking is fuzzy.

A soft wind begins to blow. Like a curtain parting, the fog opens before you. And then there it is! Before you in the jungle gloom stand hundreds of oddly lifelike statues. As you approach them, your movements become even more leaden, your breathing more labored, your mind more fuzzy.

Ponderous steps take you past statue after statue. Suddenly you recognize two of them—your brother

*Turn to the next page.*

and your father! You try to reach up to touch their faces, but it is now impossible to move your hand. It, like the rest of your body, has turned to stone. Yet you can see and think, and your heart pounds within the chest of the paralyzed, rock-hard horror you have become.

Like so many before you, you have entered the Valley of the Screaming Statues and have discovered its ugly secret. And now you, like all who have come before, are one of the keepers of this secret . . . forever. Your rigid mouth opens, and the jungle echoes with your helpless screams.

Single file, you, Chris, and Darlene make your way down to the river, and plod along the bank. Most of the time you are able to walk on damp but firm sand between the water and the jungle. But your spirits— and your energy—are beginning to sag. What has been only an hour seems like ten, and the riverbank is hot and desolate.

Suddenly you spot footprints in the sand. "People!" you exclaim, quickening your pace.

Rounding a bend, you come upon a settlement of natives working on dugout canoes, lined up in a row along the riverbank. Though startled to see you, the natives seem friendly and they come toward you. As they approach, you begin to realize there is something terribly strange about them. On each hand they have two sharp claws, instead of fingers.

Chris extends a hand, palm outward. "Give me five!" he says, grinning like an idiot.

The odd people stare at Chris, and you wish you didn't know him.

"I want to get out of here!" Darlene cries.

"You can't," says Chris. "It's not your dream."

She turns to you. "Then *you* get me out of here."

"I don't know how," you tell Darlene. You eye the natives' canoes and feel the throbbing in your feet. You have been walking a long time, and wonder

*Turn to the next page.*

what you have to offer in trade for a canoe. But already your question has been answered. The natives are studying your shoes. It seems they have never seen such things before. Just as you are about to try to communicate to the natives your idea for a trade, an old woman whose back was turned toward you slowly turns around. Her eyes are completely white. She has no pupils. Her terrifying gaze fixes on you. But it is not you the woman sees . . . it is your thoughts.

Suddenly you hear her voice inside your head, Yes, you may have a canoe for the shoes.

You turn to Chris. "She wants our—"

"Yeah, I can hear her, too," he interrupts. "She wants our shoes."

"But we need our shoes as much as a canoe," says Darlene, who has also heard the woman speaking inside her head.

"It's true," you agree, "we need both. But which do we really need the most?"

"I don't know," says Chris. "You have to decide."

*If you decide to trade the shoes for the canoe,*
*turn to the **next page**.*

*If you do not make the trade,*
*turn to **page 71**.*

Reluctantly, you take off your shoes and give them to the natives. The horrid old woman with egg-white eyes is staring into your mind again. What fools you are! her voice screeches.

Now barefoot, you, Chris, and Darlene shove a heavy dugout canoe into the river and climb aboard. As you glide along, the river changes color from moment to moment. First it is a muddy brown. Then it becomes an emerald green, which slowly turns to an inky black. Dim sunlight flickers through the trees overhead, speckling the water with tiny dots of gold.

As you marvel at this odd river, you begin to notice that it is flowing even faster, and carrying you on at an ever-increasing speed toward a fork up ahead.

Chris is pointing at the fork. "Which way?" he asks.

Shielding your eyes from the sun, you study the situation. In the left fork, the river seems to be broader and to be moving faster. The right fork seems to narrow and slow down.

"Which way?" Chris insists. "Make a decision *now!*"

*If you take the left fork,*
*turn to the **next page**.*

*If you take the right fork,*
*turn to **page 34**.*

Taking the left fork, you find that the river is a broad expanse of water so blue it looks dyed. You are surrounded by towering mountains of stone as the river, now swirling down through a gorge, moves you along at an incredible speed, out of control.

Ahead the air is like a rainbow-streaked spray. And from somewhere beyond comes a hissing roar.

"Hang on!" yells Darlene over the deafening thunder of the water.

Suddenly the river seems to collapse beneath you. The canoe shoots straight down. It slams into a trough of foam, then shoots skyward on a wave. As you catapult along, the river narrows and squeezes between steep canyon walls. You race through one horseshoe turn after another.

You, Chris, and Darlene are yelling with terror and excitement, until the "ride" ends and you glide out onto a large, smooth stretch of river.

"That was the ultimate!" exclaims Chris, turning and looking over his shoulder at you.

But you can't speak for fear of what you're seeing. Directly ahead the water drops off into space. In horror, you realize there is no way to stop the canoe as it glides relentlessly toward a giant waterfall.

Chris screams when he sees what you see. Panicked, he tries to jump from the canoe, and it tips

*Turn to the next page.*

over. You cry out as you go under the water. Gagging, you rise to the surface. But where are Chris and Darlene? They seem to have disappeared, but you have no time to deal with that. You must fight wildly against the raging torrent to keep from drowning. Despite your efforts, though, you are swept closer and closer to the brink of the waterfall.

There is no way to stop yourself and, screaming, you go tumbling over the edge into an avalanche of water. But for some reason you are falling slowly, *very* slowly. You extend your arms. You spread them like wings, and find that you are actually flying. Far below is a vast lake, and beyond that a landscape carpeted in green. You look to your right and see that Chris and Darlene have reappeared and are also flying.

"What a great dream you're having!" shouts Chris. "I could do this forever. I hope you never wake up!"

"Don't say that!" yells Darlene. "This is fun, but it's too dangerous!" She points to a grass covered plain below. "Let's land," she pleads.

Chris glides along beside you. "I want to keep flying, but Darlene might be right. Maybe it *is* too dangerous. Do you think we should land?"

*If you choose to land,*
*turn to the **next page**.*

*If you choose to keep flying,*
*turn to **page 32**.*

You swoop down low over the treetops. Smiling, you land gently on your feet on a grassy slope. Chris and Darlene stop in midair and, holding hands, descend to the ground.

In a good mood, you head off down the slope and across the plain. But soon you regret your decision to trade away your shoes. The grass makes your bare feet itch. Eventually the prickly grass does give way to barren, rocky ground, but that is worse. Now sharp stones jab and scratch your feet.

A jungle looms ahead. You enter it and finally feel relief. The ground beneath you has turned into a soggy carpet of dead leaves that feel like cool padding under your now bleeding feet.

You push along through the wet greenery, and in moments the three of you are soaked from the saunalike moisture in the air. Exhausted, you plod on, and soon an open area leads you to a vast lake with dark, gray water. It is ominous, just like your surroundings. Your only source of illumination comes from strips of light filtering through the canopy of trees overhead. As you walk cautiously on, you realize that the jungle is becoming darker, more silent, and practically airless.

Suddenly Darlene screams. You look to where she is pointing and freeze at the sight of monstrously

*Turn to the next page.*

long snakes dangling from the branches of trees that hang out over the surface of the lake. Again and again their huge, triangular heads dive under the water and swallow fish without even chewing them.

You stare at the brutes in disbelief. Their bellies wriggle with live fish kicking as they are being digested.

"Suppertime in Snakesville," Chris murmurs, trying to be funny, but clearly he, too, is disgusted by this horrid feast.

"Let's get out of here," you say, grabbing Darlene and hurrying away.

Chris, fascinated by the snakes, reluctantly follows.

Soon you discover you are on a trail. For a moment you feel better, as if the trail will lead you to safety. But then you realize the truth—you have not left the snakes behind. In fact, there are even more snakes . . . *everywhere*—wrapped around trees, coiled on rocks, and slithering through the grass.

You break into a run. But it doesn't matter how fast you to try to go   the three of you are suddenly moving in slow motion.

As if slogging through molasses, you keep going, and mercifully the brush begins to thin. Ahead there is a large clearing, and in this expanse of land is a village. From a distance it seems populated by statues. As you

*Turn to the next page.*

come nearer, you realize the statues are people, and they are moving. But if you stop, *they* stop. It is as though your arrival has set them in motion.

You hear a hissing sound coming from behind. You look over your shoulder to see more of the villagers.

"Where'd they come from?" asks Chris. For the first time, you detect a tremor of fear in his voice.

And he has good reason to be scared. The villagers behind you are opening their mouths to reveal teeth filed into points. The villagers say nothing. Instead they hiss at you . . . like snakes.

You turn to run, but which way should you go? Ahead is the village that could house who knows what kind of dangers. Behind you are the villagers, who definitely look unfriendly already. And through the jungle, to your left, there is a trail that could lead to who knows what kind of nightmare.

"What do we do?" asks Darlene, beginning to cry.

You are paralyzed with fear, but you must make a move.

*If you continue on and enter the village,
turn to the next page.*

*If you try to run away from the natives
behind you by taking the jungle trail,
turn to page 64.*

You enter the village. The natives there, like the others following you, have sharp fangs. Their clothing is made of snakeskin, and on their wrists are bracelets that make a rattling noise.

"Try not to act scared," you whisper.

"Yeah," says Chris. "We're surrounded by freaks who think they're snakes. Gee, who'd be scared?"

All around you the odd natives are hissing and rattling their bracelets. Hands push you from behind toward a large shack made of bamboo and plaited grass. Terrified, the three of you enter it.

Sitting on a throne made of bones is a man who looks to be in charge. He is a gnarled, withered little man with a bald head, but somehow he looks powerful. At his side, leaning against the throne, is a large club made of bone. He pounds the club against the floor and, hissing, gestures for you to come to him.

"He must be the chief," Chris says, pushing you forward. "Go talk to him."

As you take a step, the chief stands and comes toward you. To your surprise, he gently clasps your wrists. He says something. The words sound like hisses, but it is clear they are words of greeting. He smiles, revealing yellow teeth filed into points. Then he claps his hands together, and drums made from hollow logs begin to pound.

*Turn to the next page.*

A young woman hurries over with a large covered bowl and gives it to the chief. He lifts off the lid, and you are horrified. Inside are hundreds of tiny snakes. They are not much larger than worms, but they are definitely snakes. They coil around each other, intertwining in a writhing, ugly mass. To your disgust, the chief picks up one of the tiny, hissing creatures. He holds it up high, drops it into his mouth, and swallows.

"Gross!" exclaims Darlene.

The chief points at each of you, then points to his mouth. It is clear he wants *you* to eat a snake.

"Oh, man!" groans Chris.

"No way!" exclaims Darlene.

The smile on the chief's face disappears. He is clearly angry. He beats on the floor with his bone club. He is not asking, he is *ordering* you to eat a snake.

Hissing, the people gather around. Many have weapons. If you don't eat a snake, will they attack you? You look into the bowl of hideous reptiles. Can you eat one—especially if it means possibly saving your life? The people move closer, menacingly. The chief beats on the floor with his bone club. What will you do?

*If you refuse to eat a snake,*
*turn to the next page.*

*If you choose to eat one,*
*turn to page 30.*

You shake your head. "No, we will not eat snakes. I do not mean to offend you, but—"

He silences you by pounding his club on the floor. Burning rage fills his eyes. He hisses an order to a very ugly, very fat man. You, Chris, and Darlene are grabbed from behind by dozens of people. The fat man produces a small vial. You fight the arms that hold you, but to no avail. Your mouths are forced open. A foul-smelling, syrupy liquid is poured down your throats.

You scream and hear your friends scream. You feel as though you are burning up inside. Then as though someone flipped a switch, the world goes dark, and *within* your dream, you fall asleep.

Time passes, but how much time you don't know. It could be a thousand years or it could be a second. You awaken with a start, back into your dream. Chris and Darlene are there, too. But something is wrong. Though awake, somehow your eyes are still closed. You are looking *through* your eyelids. Chris and Darlene are also awake, seeing the world through closed eyes.

"What's going on?" asks Chris. "And where is everybody?"

You look around the shack. The natives are gone. The shack is empty . . . except for dozens of snakes

*Turn to the next page.*

dangling from the rafters. Like hot wax, a long white snake drips down from an overhead beam. It hisses and snaps at you. The snake has a human head. It is the head of the chief!

You scramble to your feet and back away. In horror, you, Chris, and Darlene, like three sleepwalkers, make your way from the hut.

Outside in various poses are the villagers. But none of them are moving. They are stiff, scale-covered statues. Snakes crawl and coil around them. Every statue is screaming; every statue is calling *your* name.

Among the screaming voices you recognize your father's and then your brother's. You race toward the statues, with Chris and Darlene in tow. But your bodies are changing. They are becoming scaly. Suddenly your arms and feet disappear. You, Chris, and Darlene are now crawling on the ground. The three of you have become snakes!

You awaken, screaming. You are in Chris Muñoz's house, and it is the middle of the night. Under a blanket, Chris is sound asleep on the couch, snoring away, and Darlene is curled up in her bright red sleeping bag. The TV is still on, and someone is talking about some corny invention he made. You turn off the TV.

Your nightmare still has you shaking, but you are relieved to be awake. It was all just a bad dream, you

*Turn to the next page.*

remind yourself, nothing more. Already, many of the details are fading away. You remember a little of the end—the worst part—where you turned into a snake.

"What a nightmare," you mutter as you groggily head for the bathroom. There you turn on the water and bend over the sink. You splash a bit of water on your face, then reach for a towel. As you dry your face, you look in the bathroom mirror. You gasp. Your face is covered with scales. Baring huge fangs, you scream.

"We've got to eat one of these snakes," you tell Darlene and Chris. "One each."

"I can't," cries Darlene.

Chris just keeps groaning and shaking his head.

"If we don't, they'll kill us," you insist.

The chief beats impatiently on the floor with his club, as if proving your point. Meeting his gaze, you pick up one of the snakes that hisses at your touch.

"It's so slimy!" Darlene wails. "I'll be sick!"

"It's better than dying," you say, putting an arm around her. "Just *do* it, Darlene. Close your eyes and don't think. OK?"

"You first," she counters.

You look from her to the tiny, hideous snake looping down from your finger. Tilting your head back, you open your mouth and let the snake drop. You chew once, twice. The taste is bitter, nauseating. You swallow, then force a smile at Chris and Darlene. "See, nothing to it."

Eyes closed tightly, Darlene shoves a snake into her mouth. Chris sighs. With a look of disgust on his face, he follows suit.

The chief nods his approval. The natives smile. Behind you, hands pat your back.

"Guess they were just testing our courage," you tell Chris. "I guess they—"

*Turn to the next page.*

A sudden shock hits you from within. You can't finish what you're saying. You feel very dizzy. You look at the chief. He seems to be a thousand miles away. He is saying something, but his words are nothing but a popping noise.

"Help me!" you cry.

Again comes the tapping on your back. You can't seem to turn around.

"Are you OK?" someone is asking. But who?

The tapping is more forceful now. You open your eyes, blink, and look up at Chris. You are in his house, curled up on top of your sleeping bag in front of the TV. Darlene is in the kitchen. She is popping popcorn.

Something hisses from behind and you nearly jump out of your skin . . . until you see the vaporizer in the room.

"My mom brought it in," Chris explains. He coughs. "I'm still trying to get over a cold."

He looks at you staring wide-eyed at the vaporizer. "What's the matter with you?" he asks. "You look like you're scared of *that*." He laughs. "Boy, and people think *I'm* strange!"

The fun of flying is just too irresistible.

"Let's fly a little longer," you call to the others.

"I'm with you!" yells Chris. He glides past you. "I'm a bird . . . I'm a plane . . . I'm—"

"You're an idiot!" Darlene laughs.

Chris ignores her and flies higher. You and Darlene follow him up through a cloud. Then you burst through the mist into glorious, bright yellow sunshine. You do cartwheels in the air, back flips, and free-falling figure eights.

Then suddenly you feel heavy, leaden. You're losing altitude. Falling in slow motion, you stare at the horrified faces of your friends. The same thing is happening to them.

"Help me!" screams Darlene. "Wh—" But her voice chokes off.

You see a change come over her. Her hair has turned into claylike strings. Her eyes, rigid with fear, look as though they are made of glass.

"Darlene!" you yell.

But she is below you, falling faster and faster. Her mouth frozen in a silent scream, she plummets toward the gorge below. And then she hits the ground, shattering into a thousand pieces like a porcelain doll.

"Darlene! Nooooo!" shrieks Chris. And then he reaches out to you. "Help me!" he begs.

*Turn to the next page.*

You grab hold of his hand, but he weighs a ton and is dragging you down. He feels and looks as if he is made of heavy, brittle clay. Still holding his hand, you try to stop your fall by jerking backward, but Chris's arm breaks off at the elbow. Horrified, you watch the rest of Chris's body tumble end over end downward. Then like Darlene, he explodes into countless pieces on the rocks below.

Gradually your fall slows, and you find yourself standing in midair. Dizzy, terrified, you stare down at the shattered pieces of your friends. Suddenly you feel something grabbing you. You look down and see you are still holding Chris's hand and arm. His stone fingers are moving! They are squeezing your hand!

"No, Chris!" you scream at the hand. "Let go!"

But the bodiless arm pulls you downward. Screaming, you hurtle toward the earth—and to your horrible death.

Taking the right fork, the river becomes narrow, listless, shallow, and choked with sandbars. Finally you grind to a halt on a clot of marshy land blocking the river. The three of you drag the heavy canoe off the sandbar, and you glide off. But it is not long before you are stuck again, and this time you have to push and pull your craft through green muck and reeds that look like long, bony fingers thrusting up from the water below.

"This place is disgusting!" groans Darlene.

"We've got to keep going," you say, digging your paddle deeper into the gooey water.

It is a relief when the river becomes clear and starts flowing again. In fact, you come upon a short set of rapids. They deliver the canoe into an orange-hued, foul-smelling mist. You pinch your nose against the stench, and for a long while travel almost blind, as though through thick gauze.

All of a sudden the mist lifts, unveiling mountains to the left and right, that appear to be covered with human skin. There are holes in this "skin," out of which huge, eyeless worms crawl.

"I can't stand it!" Darlene wails at you. "Get me out of your nightmare!"

"I'd love to," you tell her. In fact, all you want to do is wake up.

Finally you drift past the horrible mountains, and

*Turn to the next page.*

a dreary nothingness settles over everything. You continue on, silently. The heat and humidity are awful. The sun is merciless. Your bodies are bathed in putrid green sweat.

Soon the river widens, and you are paddling across a slow-moving body of water that is several miles wide. In many places it has a thin, mucuslike coating of yellow slime. There are no shores. The water simply spills out into the jungle.

You glide along, past fallen trees and heaps of rotting jungle debris. Snakes loop down from branches, drift out from dark places, and slither out along the surface. Some travel below the water, now and again raising their heads above the surface like periscopes. They do not turn their heads. They have no need to. Their heads are covered with eyes.

As some of the snakes try to slither into the canoe, you paddle faster. Soon you are free of them, and the water seems fresher, too. It is a brilliant, almost transparent blue. You are so hot and sweaty that you are tempted to dive in and go for a swim.

You look over the side of the canoe to make sure there are no snakes, and gasp in shock. Far below the surface you see what appears to be dozens of statues standing on the bottom of the lake. Their heads are turned upward as though they are looking at you.

*Turn to the next page.*

You gaze around at the steep mountainsides that surround the lake. "Maybe this used to be the Valley of the Screaming Statues," you whisper in awe, "and somehow the whole area got covered with water."

The farther out onto the lake you travel, the more statues you see. There are hundreds of them. And maybe it's your imagination, but they seem to be moving. Their heads seem to turn, their eyes following your progress. And the arms of many are extending upward, as though begging you to help them.

"Let's get out of here," you tell the others. "This place is really starting to give me the creeps."

The three of you dig your paddles in deep, working hard to make the heavy canoe move faster. Soon your hands are raw, and green sweat literally pours from you. But you are making progress. The shore is looming closer.

"Almost there!" you exclaim. "Keep paddling!"

And then a stone hand reaches up from below, grabbing the side of the canoe. The three of you bellow in terror. As though it were grasping a toy, the hand pulls down, then flips the canoe. Crying out as you hit the water, you catch a glimpse of a stone arm going around Darlene's neck, dragging her under.

Meanwhile, as Chris swims wildly toward where his sister was, a dozen stone arms wrap around him.

*Turn to the next page.*

Hands of stone are grabbing you, too. You kick and fight, but it does no good. You are dragged underwater in a deadly embrace. Your lungs are screaming for oxygen. Your head pounds. Your sight grows dim. Unable to stop yourself, you open your mouth. As you gasp for air, your lungs fill with water.

All goes black and silent as life leaves your body. And though dead, still you are somehow aware of what has happened, of what *is* happening.

The arms that embrace you relax their grip. But it makes no difference. You have turned to stone. Your weight sends you to the bottom of the lake. Not far away are Chris and Darlene, also turned to stone, frozen in place in the horrid underwater graveyard.

You hear a voice. It is close behind you—and familiar. Slowly your head of stone turns. You see the face of your father.

"You are one of us now," he says, bubbles rising from his mouth. "One of us forever."

It is too scary to go on alone. You decide to stick with Chris and Darlene. As you retrace your steps along the trail, you begin to feel guilty about stopping your search for your father and brother.

"Hey, where are we?" Chris suddenly blurts out.

Ahead, the trail ends in a thick, impassable wall of giant plants. Their stalks corkscrew upward in ugly, misshapen spirals. The leaves are colorful, huge, and triangular like sports pennants.

Chris frowns. "This is the same trail we came in on, isn't it? How did all these huge, weird plants suddenly grow here?"

You turn your head to look back down the way you just came and gasp in disbelief. The trail down which you've just walked no longer exists! Instead, a few feet ahead of you there is a sheer drop. You move carefully to the edge of the abyss and gaze down. Hundreds of feet below you can see the village you left only a short while before.

"It's not possible!" exclaims Darlene.

You look around frantically. To your left is a narrow trail you had not seen before—or that possibly had not even *been* there before. "This looks like the only way out," you tell the others.

Worried, the three of you head down the trail, plunging deep into the jungle. There are many trees,

*Turn to the next page.*

but they are bare. Their dry, white branches look like skeleton limbs, and it is obvious that they are dead. The ground is barren. But every now and then, there are rocks with strange toadstools growing out of them. The toadstools are gray, lumpish things that look like human brains.

Darlene's chin is quivering. "I want to get out of here!" she says emphatically. "I hate this place!"

"But what are we supposed to do?" you ask. "We can't head back. The trail—it's gone!"

Chris agrees and uncharacteristically tries to reassure his sister, telling her to be brave. He must be really scared.

Sidestepping the bizarre toadstool-laden rocks, you skirt through the skeleton trees, now growing more plentiful and closer together. Their bony branches intertwine overhead, and more and more you notice thick cobwebs draped all over them. Happily there seems to be no sign of spiders.

The three of you make your way across a stream into yet another forest of skeleton trees. They, too, are draped with spiderwebs: wet, shimmering, sticky-looking—and obviously fresh. Ahead there are more trees, but they look alive. Their trunks are brown, not white, and their leaves are a sickly lime green.

As you approach them, you see there is something

*Turn to the **next page**.*

odd about the bark. It looks fuzzy . . . almost hairy. Suddenly the bark starts to move, to writhe. The "bark," you realize, is nothing but thousands of tiny brown spiders. They have attached themselves to the trees and seem to be sucking the life right out of them, turning the bark from green to white.

Darlene backs away from them and shrieks. She has backed into a branch, and hundreds of swarming spiders have fallen into her hair, on her arms, and on her face. Darlene rolls on the ground, thrashing and slapping at them. You and Chris spring to her aid, crushing spiders, wiping them off her, and picking them from her hair. Though horrified by the spiders, Darlene is unhurt.

"You're all right!" says Chris, putting an arm around his sobbing sister. "Let's get out of here."

Moving slowly, carefully, so as not to disturb the spiders, the three of you retreat down what appears to be an animal trail. Everywhere curtain-size spider-webs are draped from tree to tree. You stare in disgust and disbelief. In the center of the webs are the remains of rats, panthers, monkeys—all bleached white, all looking like chalky statues.

Chris is slightly ahead of you on the trail. Suddenly he stops, pointing in horror at a giant web. There, hanging in the wispy strands, are human corpses. Like

*Turn to the next page.*

the animals, they are bleached white, as though something has drained the life from them. Their mouths are frozen open in mid-scream.

"Whatever got them might still be around," you whisper, as if whatever it was could hear you.

"Well, let's not hang around to find out," says Chris. "I don't want to end up like that!" He nods in the direction of a wrinkled-up, white statue of a man, spread-eagled in the center of a web.

"What's that?" Darlene blurts out. "I thought I heard something up there in the trees."

You pause to listen. At first you hear nothing. Then comes a hideous sound, like the clattering of thousands of tiny claws. Slowly you gaze upward toward the sound and your mouth drops open. Through the canopylike webwork of skeletal branches, there are huge, hideous spiders. They are white, blending in with the color of the branches, making them nearly impossible to see as they scramble along.

Actually, it is only their eyes and their mouths that are discernible. The eyes are yellow, bulging like frog eyes, and from their circular red mouths a single white fang alternately protrudes and retracts.

"What do we do?" cries Darlene.

"Run!" yells Chris. "Run for your life!"

"No!" you tell him. "If we run we'll attract more

*Turn to the next page.*

attention. The spiders, they'll—"

But your words of advice are lost on him. He is backpedaling, pulling on Darlene. She gazes blankly at him.

"Run!" he screeches, giving her a shove that propels her forward. She staggers. Then the two of them break into a run. There is nothing you can do but follow them. It is better than staying alone.

You struggle to catch up. Your heart races. Your breath comes in choking gasps of exhaustion and fear. Your footfalls are heavy, loud. A matting of dead, dry leaves and twigs snap and crunch beneath your feet.

There is another, even louder sound. It is coming from overhead. The monstrously large, white spiders are clattering along on the bony treetops. They are racing overhead, stride for stride with you.

Darlene and Chris have heard and seen them, too. They slow their pace, and you catch up to them.

You point through the trees. Not far ahead you can see an open meadow. "We're going to make it!" you yell, breaking into a run.

A sudden scream from Chris comes from behind you. Then a gasp. He has tripped and is on the ground, gripping his knee, crying out in pain. Darlene is huddled over him, trying to help him. She looks at you, then looks up. "No!" she yells.

*Turn to the next page.*

You gaze up in horror. A shimmery, slimy line—as thick as white nylon rope—dangles from a web . . . and on it, a monstrously huge spider is rapidly descending, its claws open, ready to pounce on Chris and Darlene.

You look around frantically for a weapon. There are large stones fairly close. Farther away, on the ground, is a long, broken-off bonelike branch. But maybe you don't even have time to go for a weapon. Perhaps it's best just to fight the spider with your bare hands.

You have only a fraction of a second to decide what to do.

*If you choose the rocks and stones,*
*turn to the next page.*

*If you choose the bony, spearlike branch,*
*turn to page 99.*

*If you choose to fight with your bare hands,*
*turn to page 114.*

The branch is too far away, you decide, and so you immediately grab a heavy stone. Raising it high overhead, you smash it down on the spider. You can't believe your eyes. The rock penetrates the spider's body and is sucked right into its flesh, as though the creature were made of some sort of horrid white pudding.

Chris and Darlene are screaming. The spider is on top of them, embracing them with its multiple legs.

You hoist an even larger stone and bellowing with rage, smash it down on the spider. This stone, too, sinks into the beast's gooey white flesh.

"Help us!" shrieks Chris.

Stumbling, you turn to get the branch, only to find your way blocked by another horrid spider! It slaps at you with a pincerlike leg, which smashes into your hip and sends you reeling. You land heavily. Struggling to your feet, you stare in disbelief at the scene unfolding before your eyes.

The first spider is holding Darlene with three of its legs while it goes to work on Chris. A transparent needlelike fang slides out from its red mouth, at which point the creature lowers its head and plunges the fang into Chris's forehead. His shrieks fill your ears as the clear needle turns red, filling with blood, with *Chris's* blood. His body goes limp, then flat, like

*Turn to the next page.*

a deflated, human-shaped balloon. Again the fang is plunged into your friend's forehead, this time injecting a chalky white liquid into Chris. His body fills, inflates, changes, then finally hardens. Chris's skin has turned to powder-white stone.

Darlene is still alive, still squirming, still crying, reaching out to you from beneath the spider's body. You grab hold of her hand . . . as you are hit from behind by the other spider. Devastated with pain, you think you might faint as it wraps you in its many-jointed arms. Instead you fight, kicking desperately, and for a moment you manage to get out from under the thing.

But backing away you step into some sort of huge, sticky net, and realize you are trapped in a massive spider web. The more you thrash and fight, the more hopelessly you become entangled.

On the ground not far from you is Chris, now hardened into a statue. More spiders descend from above. Like hairy, monstrous puppets on strings, they gather Chris up and carry him away.

Suddenly you hear a clattering sound overhead. When you look up, you see several spiders are now coming at you! Your screams of horror and fear mix with those from Darlene. She cries out your name as a spider carries her away, too. It lifts her into the air,

*Turn to the next page.*

then pins her against a tree. Again a transparent needlelike fang slides out from its mouth . . . and plunges into Darlene's forehead.

Helpless, you watch as she turns chalky white, then is carried up into the trees toward awaiting webs, one of which now houses the statuelike body of Chris.

The web holding you begins to shake and vibrate. Rolling your eyes upward, you see several spiders closing in on you. Trying to get free, you kick, squirm, twist, writhe . . .

And awaken, to find yourself tangled up in your sleeping bag in Chris Muñoz's living room!

Bathed in sweat, you untangle yourself from the sleeping bag and sit up. You are half-asleep, confused, and trembling. Though you are relieved that it was just a nightmare, relieved to be back in the real world, you are still pretty shaken up by the dream.

You glance at the windows. It's dark outside. A wind is gusting, rattling the glass panes. Your attention turns to the clock on the mantelpiece. It's 4:31 in the morning. The TV is still on. An old black-and-white scary movie is being broadcast.

You wipe sweat from your brow, relax, and almost smile. It was just a dream, and you are feeling much better now.

*Turn to the next page.*

The house is dark and quiet, lit only by the flickering light of the TV. The only sound is the eerie background music from the movie.

You turn to look behind you. To the core of your being, you are shocked, horrified. "Chris!" you shriek. "Darlene! Nooo! It can't be! No!" You stumble to your feet, staring at a statue of Chris sitting in a chair. A statue of Darlene lies sideways on the sofa.

Your mouth opens rigidly, woodenly. And the house fills with your screams.

Headed west, you come upon a red stone plateau. A hot wind gusts, blowing reddish grit into your faces. It is hard to breathe, hard to swallow.

When the wind abates, you continue on and come to a marshy area. Logs have been laid side-by-side to form a boardwalk over it. You nod toward the logs. "Must be people nearby," you say, starting across.

"I'm getting tired," says Chris. "I should have brought my dad's pickup along in your dream."

"You are *so* strange!" says Darlene, trudging after you and Chris. "You don't even know how to drive."

At the end of the boardwalk is a vast gorge, and suspended across it is a long, rickety bridge made of crude ropes and twisted vines. There is a drop of hundreds of feet to the bottom of the gorge, where a twisting river shimmers. Although it is probably huge, from such a great height it looks like a thin, clear ribbon.

"You don't expect us to cross that thing?" asks Chris, pointing to the bridge.

You study the crude, clumsy-looking bridge then gaze down into the gorge. The dizzying height makes your palms sweat with anxiety, but you must choose.

*If you decide to cross the bridge,*
*turn to the next page.*

*If you decide not to cross it,*
*turn to page 51.*

"Let's go for it," you tell the others. "People have probably been using this bridge for years."

"You first," says Chris. "If you live, then I'll go."

"Gee, what a buddy!" you scoff.

Gathering your willpower, you take your first few steps onto the bridge. Though it bounces with each footstep, it seems pretty solid. Wanting to get the scary ordeal over with as quickly as you can, you hurry along.

Suddenly there is a loud snap underfoot, and the wood beneath you collapses. In the nick of time you grab hold of a rope of twisted vines.

Now your whole life dangles on a single crude rope. You look down and see the gorge—and the river—hundreds of feet below. Desperately you try to pull yourself up, but your strength is ebbing. You feel as though your muscles are going to explode and the joints of your elbows and shoulders are going to dislocate. Your hands are sweaty. You feel yourself slipping downward. You twist, kick, and scream for the help you know your friends can't give you.

Your efforts to pull yourself up, along with the breeze, cause the rope to swing out of control. Out of the corner of your eye, you catch sight of Chris, cautiously making his way toward you. He goes to his knees, then lies down on the bridge. He reaches

*Turn to the next page.*

down to you, touching your arm. But the rope is unraveling. You are losing your grip.

Suddenly you are falling. Flailing and grasping at air, you plummet into the gorge. You close your eyes against your imminent death.

As you hear Chris calling your name from above, the rocks rush up at you from the gorge below.

Closer . . . closer.

And then you jerk awake. Chris, with his hand on your arm and a bemused expression on his face, is staring at you. You are in the Muñoz home.

You see Mr. Muñoz coming down the stairs. "Anything wrong?" he asks, taking in the situation.

"Nah, Pops," says Chris. "Someone"—he winks at you—"was just having a righteous nightmare."

"We have no way of knowing what's on the other side of the bridge," you say. "Let's not cross it."

"You're chicken," Chris sneers, then breaks into a grin. "But that's cool. I'm chicken, too."

Darlene lets out a sigh of relief.

The three of you head along the lip of the gorge, then down a long, rock-strewn slope. The farther down you go, the larger the rocks are. Many are huge and almost perfectly square. The rocks are pock-marked, too, making them look like giant dice.

The slope gradually levels off and the vegetation becomes thick. You push your way into a clearing, then pause to say something to Chris. But you stop yourself. Your mouth drops open.

Standing not twenty yards away is a man.

"Who are you?" asks Darlene fearfully.

The man looks startled, too. He turns and disappears back into the brush, returning a moment later with several other men. They have blue designs tattooed on their bodies and faces. All are barefoot and wear nothing but cloth rags. They carry long blowpipes and machetelike knives, and they appear to be on a hunting expedition.

"Hello!" you call, taking a step forward.

The men jabber among themselves in a strange language that has a harsh clicking sound. They seem

*Turn to the next page.*

to be arguing. One of the men, wearing cutoff jeans, advances toward you with his blowpipe in his mouth. The other natives scoff at him. Grumbling something angrily, he lowers the blowpipe and says something to you. You shrug, not understanding.

Now the man in cutoffs begins walking around you, as though inspecting you. He waggles the blowpipe in your face, then at Chris. The weapon has an iron point. He presses the point against Chris's chest.

"Leave my brother alone!" demands Darlene.

The man swings the blowpipe in her direction. Suddenly a gray-haired man, seemingly the leader of the group, pushes the blowpipe away. Harsh words are exchanged. There is laughter as the man with the blowpipe backs off.

The old man says something to the other natives. They begin to move off, in the direction of a trail. He gestures to the three of you to follow. Not knowing what else to do, you fall behind them and walk easily along a narrow but well-defined path.

Now and again one of the men halts and slips a dart into his blowpipe. He puts it to his lips; there is a *pffft* sound, and an animal comes tumbling down in the foliage. Rats, snakes, bats, squirrels, lizards, and monkeys—all felled by darts—go into wicker baskets the hunters have strapped to their backs.

*Turn to the next page.*

As you round a bend, you see a village in a valley below. One long, barracklike house—two hundred yards long—is surrounded by a few small huts built on piles of stone. And down on the banks of a flat, slow-moving river, there is another house, this one built on stilts. It looks nicer than the other dwellings. You notice a small motorized boat tied up to one of the stilts supporting the house.

Everyone in the village, it seems, is hurrying out to greet you. Chattering and babbling, they stop whatever tasks they were engaged in and rush toward you. Suddenly you are surrounded by what appear to be at least a hundred people, many of whom are wearing watches, tennis shoes, blue jeans, and other modern items.

A large, hulking man, wearing a sarong and white pants, emerges on the veranda of the longhouse. The people become silent, reverent, as though he is their leader. His eyes on you, Darlene, and Chris, he listens to the gray-haired hunter whisper something in his ear, then he beckons you to follow him into the longhouse.

It seems clear that the longhouse is where most everyone in the village lives. Along one wall is a very long line of private rooms, each seemingly the home of a family. All the rest of the longhouse, it appears, is given over to community activities—cooking, eating,

*Turn to the next page.*

and making handicrafts. Hanging on the walls, and from the rafters, is a vast display of weapons, utensils, and trophylike items. There are axes, blowpipes, pots of all shapes and sizes, tapestries, animal skins, and masks of carved wood.

There are also human heads on display. Most look ancient. Withered and rotting, they are blackened by smoke and caked with dust. A few look almost new— obviously more recent additions.

"Cool!" Chris exclaims. "Shrunken heads!"

"What if these guys decide to chop off *your* head?" Darlene asks, raising an eyebrow.

"That would not be cool," he replies. He is trying to act as though the question does not bother him, but fear registers as much on his face as on Darlene's. And you know you must look absolutely petrified.

Your reaction to the heads causes some of the natives to laugh. A flat-nosed man attempts a faltering explanation. He points to the heads and says, *"Dayak."* He points to himself and then to those around him in the longhouse and says, *"Kayan."*

"You are Kayan and they are Dayak?" you ask. "Dayak—?" You bring your finger across your throat in a slashing motion.

The man nods.

"But how about nice guys like us?" asks Chris.

*Turn to the next page.*

He points to himself, makes the same slashing motion across his neck. "I mean, like I'm not in the mood to be decapitated now."

The flat-nosed man smiles, shakes his head, and puts his hand on Chris's shoulder to reassure him.

A silence falls as the leader approaches. He seems angry, and rattles off a string of words at the flat-nosed man. The man bows and retreats as the chief motions for the three of you to be seated, then takes his place before you on a thickly plaited straw mat.

Standing behind you are dozens of onlookers. The leader launches into what seems to be a welcome speech. From time to time he forces a smile on his grim face, as if to help you feel comfortable.

Suddenly there is a flurry of excitement. The crowd parts as a smiling, gap-toothed man approaches. His hair and beard are long; his eyes are beady yet playful. He is wearing a plaid shirt, short khaki pants, and sandals. He looks harmless, but for some reason the natives seem fearful of him. He bows to the leader, then turns his attention to the three of you. "Well, well, well," he says, a gleam in his eyes. "What have we here?"

Relieved to hear English, you readily tell him your names.

"Damon Youngblood's my name," he says. "I'm

*Turn to the next page.*

the trader, so to speak, in these parts. I've been waiting for you for many years."

"What are you talking about?" asks Chris. "We don't even know you. So how could you have—?"

Youngblood raises his hand for silence. "I've been waiting, not to make a trade with you, but to offer you something."

"What?" you ask.

"Your father and brother."

You gasp. "You know where they are?"

"I do indeed," says Youngblood. "Come, I'll show you." He whispers something to the leader. The man argues, unleashing a harsh barrage of words at Youngblood, who sneers and aims a finger at the leader. The anger on the man's face is replaced with a look of dread. He lowers his head in fear and resignation.

Youngblood bows to the leader—contemptuously, it seems—then turns to you. "Follow me," he says, headed toward the house on stilts.

Inside, an enormous clutter of merchandise is haphazardly displayed. Youngblood pulls a box from a back shelf amidst the clutter. He produces a key from his pocket. You touch the box. It is large, made of iron, and etched with an intricate design. The hinges and keyhole are made of heavy brass.

"I thought you said you had my father and

*Turn to the next page.*

brother," you tell Youngblood.

"And indeed I do"—he pats the box—"in here."

"That's totally insane!" blurts Chris.

"How could they be in *there?*" you demand.

Youngblood chuckles, then inserts the key into the lock. It clicks and he opens the box. He pushes it across the counter for you to see. Inside the box are dozens of small, lifelike statues. They are flesh-colored, and smooth and shiny, like ivory. All have expressions of pain on their faces. You gasp at the sight of tiny statues of your brother and father. To your horror, your father's mouth opens. "Help me," he begs in a tiny voice. An ugly chorus of voices then joins his, as all the other statues clamor for help. You reach toward your father.

Youngblood shuts the box with a bang. "Not so fast," he says. "You have a choice to make."

He locks the box and puts his hand on it. In his other hand, he holds up the key. "You can have the key *or* the box, but not both."

"If I don't have the box, what good is the key?" you ask. "And without the key, the box is useless."

Youngblood smiles. "Exactly. Now choose."

*If you choose the box,*
*turn to the next page.*

*If you choose the key,*
*turn to page 61.*

You look Youngblood in the eye. "I want the box," you say with conviction. "I'll find some way to open it."

Youngblood flashes an evil smile, laughs, then pushes the box across the counter. You reach for it. But suddenly you feel ill. The box was close enough for you to have reached it, but now it is above you, beyond your grasp. In horror, you look down at yourself.

"Help me!" you cry. "I'm shrinking!" You look up at Darlene and Chris. They seem like giants.

"What did you do to my friend?!" you hear Chris demand of Youngblood. His voice is so loud it sounds as though it has been shot out of a cannon.

"I did nothing," says Youngblood. "It was your friend's choice." He points to Chris and Darlene. "In fact, he has chosen the same fate for you as well."

"What do you mean?" Chris asks fearfully.

Looking up from your shrunken state, you see a giant Chris and Darlene getting smaller and smaller.

They try to run, but their legs, despite all their efforts, are tiny little things and carry them only a few feet. Little by little, they slow down, then come to a stop, frozen in place.

Youngblood's laughter is so loud your eardrums feel as though they'll burst. You try to cover your ears, but your arms won't move. Slowly, painfully,

*Turn to the next page.*

you crane your neck to gaze up at Youngblood.

He is leering down at you.

"You monster!" you say, your voice a feeble squeak.

Again he laughs.

Inch by inch, agonizingly, you look down at yourself. Like Chris and Darlene, you are miniaturized, rigid, and fixed in place.

Booming, crunching footsteps approach. A huge hand—Youngblood's—reaches down and picks you up. With his other hand he picks up Chris and Darlene. He places the three of you on the countertop, then inserts the key into the lock on the box. There is an ear-splitting metallic click. The box opens. Youngblood snatches the three of you up, puts you in the box, and then shuts the lid.

In the dark of the box, with Darlene, Chris, and the other statues, you hear Youngblood laughing. Then you feel the box moving as it is picked up. You and the other statues are jostled inside as the box is carried off. You topple over one another, all of you screaming and begging for help. Again, Youngblood laughs. You hear a horrid scraping noise, and guess the box has been slid back onto the shelf.

Lying on your side in the dark, you can barely make out the other statues. Close by, you can see the dark outline of Darlene, her face frozen in grotesque

*Turn to the next page.*

terror. But Chris is nowhere in sight, nor are your father or brother. You call their names over and over, but there is no answer. One of the other statues tells you to be quiet. "We have all been screaming for years," it tells you. "It never does any good."

You lay there quietly in the dark. And there you will remain, you now realize, forever.

"I think I should take the key," you tell the others.

"How come?" asks Darlene.

"I'm not sure, except I think that's the opposite of what Youngblood expects me to do."

"Well, I hope it's the right choice," says Chris.

You turn to Youngblood. "I want the key," you tell him, trying to sound brave.

Youngblood hands it to you, an odd smirk on his face.

"I want the key, because I think—"

You are unable to finish what you were about to say. You suddenly feel as if your body has been split into a thousand pieces, and somehow you are falling—*upward*—into darkness. You are tumbling, rolling over and over. You are being pulled, *sucked*, through a seemingly endless black tube of space, a tunnel where up is down and down is up.

Somewhere in the tunnel you see a second image of yourself. You and your twin pass in the dark. You drift apart, spiral away, and disappear in a timeless black nothingness.

Then, racing toward you, you can see the end of the tunnel. A speck of light, a dot of illumination, a circle of growing brightness awaits you.

Finally you are no longer moving. Only the tunnel moves. It is receding, moving away from you,

*Turn to the next page.*

closing behind you, and vanishing.

You feel your feet on solid ground. For a long moment your sight is blurred. Then your eyes begin to focus. You gaze out across an endless, barren landscape.

As far as the eye can see there is nothing but a seemingly limitless slab of smooth marble. Ahead there is a slight rise, and set in the marble is a massive stone door with a large metal lock.

As if drawn by a magnet, you move automatically toward it. You insert the key in the lock, turn it, and find yourself entering the Muñoz home. The door slams shut behind you. Slipping the key into your pocket, you walk into the living room, and there you see three sleeping forms. Chris is curled up under a blanket on the couch; Darlene is in her sleeping bag; and *you* are asleep on yours.

Fascinated, you approach this sleeping twin of yourself. You reach down to touch it, to see if it is real. Your hand passes right through, and you feel yourself merging with your own body. You roll over . . . and open your eyes.

It is the middle of the night and you are lying on top of your sleeping bag. Chris and Darlene are sound asleep.

Boy, what a weird dream, you tell yourself. Groggy,

*Turn to the next page.*

rubbing your eyes, you stand up, and stretch. You go to the front door and open it, checking to make sure you're back in reality.

You step out into the cool night. Most of the houses are dark, though some have porch lights on. Somewhere a cat lets out a screech and a dog starts barking. A car passes down the street, its headlights piercing the night like knives of light.

Because it is chilly, you stuff your hands in your pockets and are surprised to feel metal. A strange feeling sweeps over you as you pull out the key the trader gave you in what you thought was only a dream.

If not a dream, then what was it? you wonder. Where was I while I slept? And how do I return there?

But with a sinking feeling, you realize that there is no way back, and you will never see your brother and father again. For without your dream, the key you hold in your hand is useless.

You stare at the snake people. Anything has to be better than *them*. "Run for it!" you yell, jagging left down the trail, with Chris and Darlene on your heels.

Behind you, the natives let out exclamations of anger. Then a barrage of arrows zing and zip through the air, impaling plants and trees, skittering off rocks all around you.

"I've been hit!" yelps Chris, shaking blood off his hand where an arrow has grazed him.

"Hang in there!" you yell, urging him on.

"I'm OK," he says, huffing and panting, barely managing to keep up with you and Darlene.

The three of you round a bend into thicker, darker vegetation. Black moss hangs down like hair from the long limbs of massive trees. The stuff whips across your face and body as you make your way as fast as you can down the trail, while gnarled roots and creepers threaten to trip you at every step.

Ahead the path opens up, then splits. One way leads downhill but is muddy. The other way is dry but uphill. You have only a fraction of a second to decide.

*If you go downhill,*
*turn to the next page.*

*If you go uphill,*
*turn to page 93.*

"Go downhill!" you yell to the others. And you, Darlene, and Chris are off down a muddy path so steep and slippery that when Chris stumbles into you and Darlene, the three of you fall, slipping and sliding down the mucky trail, unable to stop or even slow yourselves.

"What is that?" Chris cries out, pointing ahead as you careen down the hill.

Below is a strange wall of blackness, and you are shooting straight for it. Faster and faster you hurl down the slick trail, until suddenly you come to an abrupt stop . . . *inside* the black wall.

"Where are we?" you hear Darlene ask.

"What happened?" asks Chris.

"Don't know," you gasp, wiping mud off yourself.

Suddenly you hear shouting and then sliding and tumbling sounds. It is the natives, coming down the muddy path.

"Keep going!" yells Chris. "They're still after us!"

You try to run, but you, Chris, and Darlene keep tripping and falling in the darkness. You stumble on, you arms straight out in front of you, feeling your way as if you were blind.

Behind you, footsteps crunch. It is the natives, moving in relentlessly, trying to hunt you down in the dark jungle.

*Turn to the next page.*

The three of you hurry on, pushing through foliage you cannot see. The jungle begins to thin, and you are walking on soggy, mucky ground. It seems you are in a swamp of some kind. In some places you are ankle-deep in muddy water. The three of you slosh along—with no idea where you are going.

A hand suddenly touches you, holding you back.

"Quiet," whispers Chris. "Shhh. Listen."

You hear the slapping splash of many feet, but this time the sound is receding. The natives are headed away from you.

"They're bugging out," says Chris.

"Maybe they've got a reason," says Darlene. "Maybe they know something dangerous is ahead—something we don't know about."

"They're probably heading back toward the light," says Chris. "They know how to get back, but we don't. Should we follow them?" he asks you. "I mean, I don't want to be killed by them, but I don't want to stay here in the land of perpetual nighty-night."

"What should we do?" Darlene asks.

*If you decide to take your chances in the dark, turn to the **next page**.*

*If you choose to follow the natives out of the dark, turn to **page 87**.*

"There's no way I'm going to follow those fang-toothed creeps," you tell you friends. "I'd rather take our chances in the dark. It's bound to get light sometime, right?"

"But we could walk right over a cliff without seeing it," complains Darlene. "Could we at least hold hands?"

"So if one of us goes over a cliff, we all go?" Chris sneers.

"No, stupid, so that we don't get separated," Darlene snaps back.

"Darlene's right," you say. "We need to stay together."

And with that, before Chris can protest, you grab his hand with your left hand and Darlene's hand with your right, then head off into the ink-black darkness.

As you walk along, the water you are slogging through becomes deeper. It is now up to your waist, sometimes rising almost up to your shoulders. Soon the water is over your heads, and the three of you are forced to swim in black water in a black world.

And then . . . your foot hits something. "Land!" you yell happily. Exhausted, you lumber out of the water and, dropping to your knees, you sift your fingers through cool, dry sand. Although you are still enveloped in total darkness, and although every

*Turn to the next page.*

muscle in your body is aching, you lay back on the sand and, for a brief moment, relax.

"Oh, man, I'm wiped out," Chris moans.

You turn your head and look in the direction of his voice. You see only a feeble outline of him, a silhouette of black on black. Shivering in your wet clothes, you curl into a ball on your side. Fighting sleep, you drift off, jerk awake, then drift off again.

Finally you can fight it no longer and you let yourself sleep . . . for eight hours. Or is it eight minutes? Or eight seconds?

You open your eyes. You squint, realizing that bright, glaring sunlight has awakened you. Chris and Darlene are asleep on the sand next to you. You nudge them awake. Using your hands to shield your eyes from the blazing sun, you see that you are on an island surrounded by a boundless sea.

"How did we get here?" asks Darlene, still sleepy.

"I haven't got a clue," you say, scrambling to your feet to have a look around.

In one direction across low-lying sand is a strange, hook-shaped beach that juts out into a lagoon. Scattered over it are squarish white rocks. Green-yellow seaweed is wedged between the gaps. It all looks like a giant set of dentures with spinach between the teeth.

*Turn to the next page.*

Behind you is a knoll, a low hill that blocks your view of the other side of the island. Chris scrambles to the top of the knoll, and you and Darlene follow close behind.

"Awesome!" he yells, pointing to a rusting wreck of a ship.

Stern-first, the old ship is wedged into a mass of jagged, half-submerged black rocks for most of its length, some two to three hundred yards from shore.

"Sunken ships are so totally cool," you say. "Maybe we can swim out to it."

"Yeah," exclaims Chris. "There's probably lots of weird stuff inside."

"But it's so far," Darlene says. "I mean, can we swim all that way? What if we drown?"

"Drowning causes death, as I understand it," says Chris. "Drowning is not a good thing. One must avoid drowning, whenever possible."

"Very cute," says Darlene. "And what about sharks, or undertow, or—?"

Chris adjusts his glasses and assumes the manner of a big-shot scientist. "Not to worry," he tells Darlene. "It is known that in this part of the ocean, whatever ocean this may be, there are only vegetarian sharks, who snack exclusively on seaweed, pasta, and lawn clippings."

*Turn to the **next** page.*

You snap your fingers in front of Chris's face. "I hate to interrupt your intriguing dissertation, but can we get back to reality for a moment?"

Chris shrugs. "Sure, whatever that is."

"The question is," you say, trying to get back on track, "do we try to swim out to the ship or not?"

"Well, I'd like to explore it," Chris says, grinning.

"And I'd like to stay alive," Darlene says, frowning. What are *you* going to do?

*If you decide to explore the wrecked ship,*
*turn to page 79.*

*If you decide not to swim out to the ship,*
*turn to page 101.*

"OK," you tell Chris. "We need our shoes to protect our feet. Besides, I'm not so sure we can even handle one of these heavy old canoes."

You turn to the woman with white, pupil-less eyes. "I'm sorry," you say, "but we can't make the trade."

Her thoughts bore into your head: You are a fool. I knew you were not going to make the trade even before you did.

You shake your head, as if trying to shake the old woman's thoughts out. "This old woman's really freaking me out," you tell Chris and Darlene. "I say we jam out of here."

The three of you hurry off, leaving the old woman and the weird natives with clawed fingers behind.

You'll be sorry, you hear the woman's voice in your head as you make your way along a ledge above the river.

The bank becomes steeper, and it is taking you higher above the river and farther inland. You walk for what seems like hours, but since none of you has a watch, you don't know for sure how long it's been.

"I'm getting hungry," says Darlene.

"There's probably a fast food drive-thru up ahead," jokes Chris. "They're everywhere."

You are hungry, too, but try to concentrate on keeping your footing. You are now very high above

*Turn to the next page.*

the river, and often you can't even see it.

The trail is becoming narrower and is often clogged with vegetation. You backtrack, then take a side trail down a rocky slope. It appears to be an animal trail. You can see many paw and hoof prints, and now and again there are human footprints . . . at least they *seem* human.

Suddenly Darlene stands rock-still. "What's that hissing sound?" she says, her voice shaking.

You had been looking intently at the ground, not paying much attention to anything else. Now you hear the hissing, too. You also hear a soft pattering. Then suddenly you see what looks like a block of rain coming toward you. It is all falling in one place. Like a moving drapery of water, it is bearing down on the three of you at a steady clip.

"I don't like the looks of that stuff," says Chris. "Anybody got a raincoat?"

"It's just a little water," says Darlene. "It can't hurt you."

"But it looks weird," says Chris, "and it's heading for us fast. I say we run."

*If you disagree with Chris and
don't run from the rain,
turn to the next page.*

*If you agree with Chris and run from
the rain, turn to page 75.*

"Well, *I* say we swim," you declare, trying to joke.

As you speak, the curtain of water lowers on you. First, it is a drizzle. Then a downpour. Then a deluge. And finally a flood.

If it hadn't lasted for only a few seconds, the three of you might have drowned. Instead, you are just soaked to the skin.

"See, it was just water," sputters Darlene.

But Chris is grimacing, as though in pain. "I don't feel so good," he whines.

The hot sun is beating down on him, causing steam to rise from his body. It is clouding up from his hair, his clothes, his skin. It looks like smoke, as though he's on fire. You are mesmerized by this, until you feel a pain in your right arm. You look down and see that it is, well, gooey. You touch it, and to your horror, a shimmering glob of flesh slides from your arm like jelly and drops to the ground.

"Arrrgh!" you bellow in terror, and then your stomach heaves.

Darlene, who had been wringing out her long hair, looks up. "What's wrong?" she asks, and then she notices that her hair is melting in her hands.

Chris is no better off. His face has turned into an ugly, puckering mass of tissue, sliding, slipping, and sloughing from his face.

*Turn to the next page.*

"The rain is melting us!" Darlene cries. And then, with hands like wet clay, she pulls out her eyebrows. Terrified, she drops them to the ground. And as she opens her mouth to scream again, all of her teeth clatter to the ground. Her body falling apart, Darlene starts running away.

Frantically Chris grabs her arm to stop her, but just stands there dumbfounded when his sister's limb comes off in his hand.

You are watching all this, and as you try to put your right ear back on, your left one falls off. You, like Chris and Darlene, are literally falling to pieces!

Consumed in your own individual horrors, the three of you are too busy to notice an assemblage of skeletons coming toward you from the hills. As they converge on you, they are whispering, *Welcome, welcome, welcome,* as if in a chant.

As you look at your friends, and then down at yourself, you realize why they are welcoming you. It seems you have become one of them. You, too, are a living skeleton, standing in a grotesque pool of your own melted flesh.

"No sense in getting soaked," you say. "I'm outta here!"

The three of you run down a slope toward a valley. You stop for a moment to watch the weird rain and see that it has stopped in one spot—the exact spot where you stood just moments before. All around the rain, you see sunshine.

"*Very* strange!" Chris mutters.

"I think it's sort of neat," says Darlene.

"Neat *and* strange," you add as the three of you continue to make your way through your nightmare, wondering what bizarre thing you will come upon next.

After a while your curiosity is answered when you see a creature run across the trail.

"Did you see that?" you ask.

The others shake their heads no.

The creature darts by again, coming from the opposite direction, but this time it stops and stares at you and your friends.

In a state of wonderment, you find yourself staring at what appears to be a man with no arms . . . and *four* legs. You are speechless. The man looks like a British gentleman, dressed in an old-fashioned suit, complete with pocket watch and fob, ascot and stickpin, and even a monocle! His shoes—all four of

*Turn to the next page.*

them—are of soft, green velvet. "Oh, oh my my my my," says the man. "Oh, my goodness!"

"Yeah, oh *my* goodness!" says Chris, finally seeing him.

You are taken aback, not only by the man's four legs and odd attire, but also by the fact that he is talking in an old-fashioned form of English, like the kind that might have been spoken in Britain back in the 19th century.

"Well, pip, pip, hup," says the man, extending a foot. "My name is Leander. And dare I ask what your names are?"

You each shake the man's foot and you tell him your names. As you do this, you notice his eyes are fixed on your arms.

"Oh, dear me, forgive me for staring," says the man, "but I have never seen one of your kind before."

"You've never seen a human?" asks Darlene.

"I have heard tales that . . . um . . . 'people' such as yourselves exist. And once, not long ago, I even heard it said that a small band of your kind with those"—he points to your arms—"things were in this very jungle. They were asking about some valley of statues or some such thing."

"The Valley of the Screaming Statues?" you ask eagerly.

*Turn to the next page.*

The man's eyes light up. "Yes!" he exclaims. "That was it." As he speaks, he spots a large toad, stomps down on it with one foreleg, and gobbles it up. With yellow frog blood still dribbling down his chin, he pins another toad and offers it to you.

"No, I think I'll pass," you tell him. "But I would like to hear more about this valley where you saw the people with *these.*" You point to your arms and smile. "You see, I'm looking for the Valley of the Screaming Statues myself."

"Well, look no farther," Leander declares. He waves two of his legs in the air as if gesturing all around him.

The three of you turn and look about . . . then gape in amazement. The landscape, which had been there before, is gone. The vegetation around you instantly hardens. All over the place mountains of stone have appeared.

"Hey, what happened?!" you yell, turning back to Leander.

But he is gone. Instead his voice thunders majestically in the air. "This *is* the Valley of the Screaming Statues."

"Come back!" demands Chris. "You can't just leave us here!"

There is no response. No voice. No sound.

*Turn to the next page.*

But then you see him. Leander is *part* of the mountain, encased in it with hundreds of other creatures. Some have four legs and no arms. Some are animals. And some are humans. They are all made of stone, and their mouths are fixed open in silent screams.

You search for the faces of your father and brother. Finally you find your father, and when you reach up to touch him, he yells, "Don't!"

But it is too late. You have already learned what he was trying to warn you about—that if you touch the stone, that is exactly what you will turn into. You feel yourself being absorbed into the mountainside. Slowly, as you become one with the stone, you try to open your mouth to warn Chris and Darlene. "Don't touch the—"

But it is too late. They have rushed up to you, and in their efforts to free you, they, too, have been sucked into the side of the mountain, their arms, legs, torsos, and faces—like yours—rendered into grotesque eternal additions to the hideous mosaic of petrified life.

"Yeah, let's go see what's in that old wreck," you say. "Last one there is a rotten sock!"

The three of you plunge into the gently lapping surf and begin swimming toward the old ship. As you approach the coral reef, the water is suddenly rougher, darker, and colder. You struggle against it, and with great effort you slowly close in on the wreck.

But the nearer you get to it, the more grotesque and uninviting it seems. It is rusted, crushed stern-first onto a permanent docking of jagged, slime-covered rocks.

The three of you pause for a moment, treading water.

"It looks scary," Darlene says, her words coming out in gasps as she tries to keep up with you and Chris, now breaststroking toward the ship. Its bulk blots out the sun, casting a giant shadow across the sea.

"This thing's been here for a long time," says Chris, grasping a half-submerged handrail and pulling himself aboard the wreck. Crawling on hands and knees, he turns, extends a hand, and helps both you and Darlene from the water.

For several minutes you rest, sitting together on the iron hull. As small waves lap against your feet, you study the wreck.

Much of the deck is rotted. Rust has eaten some

*Turn to the next page.*

of the bulkheads to a papery thinness. Those parts of the ship nearest the water are blackish green and slick with what looks like a combination of algae and oil. Other areas of the ship, especially those highest above the water, are in much better shape, though quite rusted.

With the ship almost completely on its side, the hull now serves as a floor for you. You come to a jumble of twisted steel beams and, crawling over them, you find yourself once again on a stretch of wood decking. You come to a door. Lying nearly flat, it is a hatch cover leading below.

Together the three of you wrestle it open, and you peer down a short passageway. Helping each other, you scoot down it into the amber half-light of what had once been a cabin.

Inside you find moldering boots and clothing, broken cups and plates, bottles, bedding, even the bent and rusted remains of an ancient typewriter. Because of the ship's tilt, what was once the floor now looks like a wall, and the tables and bunks in the cabins stand out in sharp contrast. All are bolted down at right angles, seeming to defy gravity.

Darlene picks up a soggy newspaper. "It's in Japanese," she says. "And look at the date—the year is 1943. This ship is from World War II!"

*Turn to the next page.*

Excitedly the three of you plow through more debris as you pass through cabin after cabin. All are the same, but the bunk in one catches your eye. It is curtained off by a filthy, ragged cloth.

Somehow you know what you will find behind it . . . but you *have* to look. Your heart racing, you pull back the curtain and gasp as you stare at a skeleton, still tucked beneath a mossy-looking blanket. On one of the bony fingers is a large ring in the shape of intertwined serpents. Should you take the ring? Quickly you decide against it.

You examine the skeleton. Partly under the skull is a plastic box wrapped with layers of tape. All over it is a coating of waxy candle droppings.

You take a deep breath and, gritting your teeth, slide the box out from under the skull. "Hey, you guys. Look what I found," you call to Chris and Darlene, rummaging in other parts of the ship.

They come scrambling over.

"Wow!" Chris says. He produces a rusty old dagger. "And I found just the thing to pry it open with."

Within minutes the latch on the old box gives way. Inside is a small notebook.

"Looks like a diary or a journal," says Darlene.

"It probably is," you say, turning the pages. "But it's in Japanese. I can't read a word of it."

*Turn to the next page.*

You put the diary next to the skeleton's hand, then the three of you continue through the dark, gloomy interior of the ship. "Hey, look at this!" you exclaim, pointing across the ship. "Bullet holes!"

"Guess the ship was in a battle or something," says Chris. He points upward. "Look at that crater in the ceiling, like there was some kind of explosion."

Farther along, there is more evidence that the ship had been attacked. A whole section where a bulkhead once was is now buckled and collapsed.

"Bombs hit this ship big time," you say. "I'll bet the captain grounded it on the island so it wouldn't sink. And the few survivors, like that skeleton dude in that bunk, probably died of starvation or thirst."

"Sounds reasonable," says Chris, kicking open a rusted door. "As reasonable as anything we've seen so far." He ducks into a room. "Hey! Anybody hungry?" You and Darlene follow Chris into what had once been a galley, or kitchen. Horrified, you suck in your breath as you find yourself surrounded by skeletons—many of whose bones are charred.

Darlene calls you and Chris over. She is standing near a twisted support beam. Sitting back to back, tied with wire to the beam, are three skeletons, burned and broken like the other skeletons, but smaller—especially one of them.

*Turn to the next page.*

"Man, let's get out of this place," says Chris. "All these skeletons are giving me the creeps."

"I thought you liked gross stuff," says Darlene.

"Yeah, well, not *this* gross! Let's go—" But Chris doesn't finish his sentence. "Hey," he whispers, "Someone's talking above in . . . *Japanese.*"

With Chris leading the way, you head up long, winding metal steps. And as you do, the ship suddenly feels like it is moving. The three of you pull yourselves outside onto the ship's deck and stare in disbelief at a group of Japanese sailors confronting you!

"Who—who are you?" cries Darlene. Her chin is quivering and her eyes are wide. You have never seen anyone look so afraid, so confused.

You share her feelings and obviously so does Chris. He looks so totally baffled and shocked; you wonder if he will lose his mind.

The sailors have closed in on you. They are screaming at you, and some are pushing you. One has taken out a pistol and is pointing it in your faces.

But you are not looking at the gun. You are looking out to sea. The ship is now sailing at quite a clip, cutting a huge, V-shaped swath through the water.

Suddenly a hand-cranked alarm begins to wail. For the moment, you are forgotten as the men begin to run in every direction. Several jostle each other in a frenzy

*Turn to the next page.*

and settle in behind an anti-aircraft gun. The weapon is pointed upward, into a pastel-blue sky filled with puffy white clouds. You look up and see fighter planes—*American* planes—going into a dive, coming straight at the ship, machine guns blazing!

"We're in the middle of a battle!" you shout. "A battle that took place during World War II!"

You hear the whining shriek of a plane, then look up to spot a dive-bomber streaking down at the ship. From the underbelly of the plane, a bomb comes tumbling. It looks as though it is coming straight at you but then falls out of sight, somewhere behind you, and you hear an explosion in the sea. Turning, you witness an amazing geyser bloom up from the water.

Then suddenly an anti-aircraft gun firing from the ship knocks a wing off the plane, and like a broken toy it tumbles into the sea. A shout of exultation and triumph rises from the sailors, but instantly changes to screams of horror and pain as a bomb rips through the foredeck, shredding metal and sending metal splinters and searing plumes of flame in every direction.

The ship has been badly damaged—riding low in the water, it seems to be on the verge of sinking. A square-jawed, rugged Japanese man in a captain's uniform barks an order and the faltering ship changes direction, heading toward an island.

*Turn to the next page.*

In all the terrible confusion, little attention has been paid to the three of you. But now all eyes again are turned in your direction. You, Chris, and Darlene are shoved forward, pushed through a doorway, and then made to go back down the metal stairs.

Once again you enter the galley—but now it looks relatively new and orderly, not the ruined, burned-out area you had seen earlier. Japanese sailors pull your hands behind your back and tie you, Chris, and Darlene back to back against a support beam.

Chris complains that the wire they used is cutting into his flesh. A man reaches down to loosen the binding, and you notice the ring on his finger. It has the same odd design of two intertwined serpents you saw on the skeleton's hand.

"Chris!" you gasp. "Darlene! Do you see what's happening to us and what's *going* to happen to us?"

"Oh, man," Chris groans. "Time is all twisted around. We went back into the past—but *now* it's all moving forward, and history is repeating itself."

Your eyes are on the man wearing the serpent ring. You watch as he yells something then runs from the galley into another part of the ship.

"He's probably going back to his bunk," says Chris.

"Yeah," you agree. "The same bunk I found him in before . . . as a skeleton!"

*Turn to the next page.*

"And the island we're headed toward," says Darlene, "is the island we were on."

"Only the ship isn't there yet," you say, picking up her train of thought, "because we're back in time, headed toward the island where the ship grounds itself, and then gets hit by a bomb, and—"

You stop yourself, as you hear the fearsome whine of a plane, plunging straight down, then pulling up. That's when you hear another sound— the whistling whine of a bomb . . . and you know it's coming straight at the ship.

"If those guys know the way out of this black hole, then I say we follow them," you tell your friends.

Chris and Darlene reluctantly agree, and together the three of you turn and follow the slapping patter of dozens of feet. You keep a safe distance, stopping now and then to listen and make sure you don't lose them.

After a while, the spattering sound changes to the cracking of twigs, the slapping of leaves, and the crunching and snapping of branches. The ground beneath you is finally dry, and you, like the natives, are making your way through jungle terrain.

Still the darkness has not lifted, and the jungle sounds and smells that surround you are doubly frightening. You can feel and touch everything, but you cannot see it, not *any* of it. There is not so much as a glimmer of light, not even the gray haze of a shadow. Never before have you seen such darkness. It is a blackness far beyond the color black.

The ground slopes upward and you pick and pull your way along, carefully supporting yourself with what you hope are branches and vines. In the dark, the vines feel like snakes, the bark of trees like hairy fur. Each time you touch something it sends shivers down your spine.

The natives are still ahead of you; you constantly worry that one or more of them has stopped and is

*Turn to the next page.*

lurking in the bushes, in the pitch dark, waiting to attack you.

Suddenly a hand touches your face! A shock wave of fear courses through you.

"It's me," says a hushed voice. "Darlene."

"What the—?" you begin to whisper.

But her hand goes to your mouth, silencing you. The two of you, now joined by Chris, listen. There are only a few footsteps ahead, *far* ahead. And then there is nothing, no sound except for a black wind rustling black leaves all around you.

"Where'd they go?" whispers Darlene.

"They're ditching us," Chris responds angrily.

"I'm not so sure if they were ever really leading us," you point out. "Anyway, we have no choice but to keep going until we reach some kind of light."

As if you had just made a wish, a warm glimmering of light passes over your hands. They tingle. Then, almost in the same instant, you have the same sensation in your legs, then on your face. You take a single step and emerge out of the darkness into the light. Right behind you, Darlene and Chris emerge, too.

Squinting into the brightness, the three of you wait for your eyes to adjust, then you look around to discover that you are standing at the foot of a steep, grassy jungle slope in a quiet valley. If the natives are

*Turn to the **next** page.*

anywhere around, in the trees or high grass, you cannot see them.

Behind you is the great wall of incredible blackness you just left. It scintillates, seems to quiver and ripple with a life of its own. It has no end, no top, and no bottom. Amazed, you reach out to it, but your hand stops as though you are touching black glass.

"Strange!" says Chris, also running his hand along the black wall. "We just came out of there!"

Tense, still watchful, you make your way along a grassy knoll that skirts the blackness. The knoll flattens then becomes a depression that leads down into a winding valley. You stop in awe.

"This is it," you tell the others, pointing at the incredible sight before you. "The Valley of the Screaming Statues."

Ahead of you, looking like a fallen army, are hundreds of stone humans. Most lie on the ground, in awkward positions, their arms and legs akimbo. Sticking in many, you can see arrows and spears all turned to stone like the bodies they pierce. Stone hammers and clubs lie strewn on the ground. And on all the statues are scrapes, cuts, and scars—etched into the flesh of stone.

Speechless, the three of you wander amid the statues, examining them. You are looking for your

*Turn to the next page.*

father and brother, but Chris and Darlene are simply intrigued and fascinated by what they see.

As you make your way far down into the valley, there are fewer and fewer statues. Soon the way ahead narrows, leading to a steep, almost vertical drop. It is too dangerous to proceed, so the three of you head back up through the valley, back past the statues, in the direction of the black wall.

You are nearing the wall, almost at it, when suddenly you stop. Your eyes open wide in disbelief.

Lying on the ground is a statue of your father. There is a stone spear through his chest, the shaft of which he is clutching . . . with hands of stone.

Not far from him, you spot your brother. He, too, is made of stone. A large cut is in his skull, and the stone hatchet that caused the wound lies nearby.

Why hadn't you seen them before? It's as if they crawled out of the pile of scattered bodies to—

"Duck!" Chris screams, startling you and breaking your train of thought.

You fall to the ground just as a fusillade of arrows whizzes by. Darlene and Chris have taken cover in a small cluster of trees. You crawl over to join them.

"We've been ambushed!" Chris whispers.

He is right. All around you in tall grass on the hillsides—grass that once looked so peaceful, serene,

*Turn to the next page.*

and empty—countless native warriors have appeared. It almost seems as though they have sprouted up out of the ground.

But you have no time to figure out where they came from. At any moment, you are sure, one of you will be hit by the innumerable spears and arrows raining down on you.

"Come on!" yells Chris, making a run for it.

But you and Darlene stay in place, watching in horror as Chris yelps in pain, staggers, then tries to reach around and pull out an arrow that has hit him in the back.

Wide-eyed, he stares in your direction, then he goes down. The transformation is sudden and complete: He and the arrow that has impaled him turn to stone in what seems like seconds.

"Chris!" you scream. Then you look at Darlene, paralyzed with fear. "There must be something—a poison—on the points of the arrows and spears," you tell her. "We can't let one of them hit us!"

Darlene, sobbing, opens her mouth as if trying to say something, but nothing comes out. A spear splinters a tree beside her, just inches from her head. She grabs your hand. "Please," she cries, tugging on you. "Let's get out of here!"

"No," you say firmly. "We're sure to end up like

*Turn to the next page.*

Chris if we try to run for it."

"Wake up!" Darlene yells at you. "If we can get back inside that wall of darkness, they won't be able to see us."

"But it's a solid wall," you argue.

She continues to pull at you, and as she does you notice how large her hand is. In fact, it is not a little girl's hand; it's—it's Mrs. Muñoz's hand!

"Wake up," she says, gently pulling your arm, helping you ease out of your sleeping bag. "Poor thing, you're having an awful dream."

"Yeah," Darlene says, standing next to her mother. "I couldn't wake you, so I got my mom."

"Why don't you go sleep in Chris's bed?" suggests Mrs. Muñoz. "Looks like he's out for the duration, and there's no sense disturbing him."

You glance at your friend sleeping heavily on the couch, still as a stone.

"Go uphill!" you shout without hesitation. Your arms pumping, your feet digging in, your heart pounding, you race up the steep grade with Chris and Darlene close on your heels.

Just as you're sure your heart will burst and you won't make it to the top, the grade of the trail finally levels out. In fact, it is almost completely flat now, as well as broad and shadowed by a massive canopy of trees. Oddly some of the trees are joined at the trunk. And overhead the branches of trees from opposite sides of the road intertwine to form a huge, single branch.

Suddenly a butterfly—or what seems to be several butterflies—flutter past your face. Somehow they, too, are all joined together, their wings, bodies, and legs forming a large flying mass resembling a multicolored floral bouquet.

You have no time to stop and admire the beauty and wonder of all that is around you, for the natives are close behind, their heavy footfalls causing the ground beneath your own feet to tremble.

"Got to keep going," gasps Chris. He is huffing, out of breath, exhausted—as are both you and Darlene.

Now the grade takes a sharp rise uphill again. It is worse than before. Every fiber of muscle in your body is throbbing. You give it everything you've got,

*Turn to the next page.*

and finally reach the crest of the hill.

If only for a moment, the three of you must rest. But then you see the natives have closed ranks. They seem to be running, step for step, with each other, their bodies so close together it is almost as if they are a single being.

You haul yourself forward along with Chris and Darlene. But you are too weak to go on. Exhausted, you stagger and fall.

Chris and Darlene pull you to your feet. With their help you manage to keep moving, and even to gain strength . . . until you look over your shoulder and see a sight so frightening your knees buckle.

The troop of natives has become one giant, massive body, thundering after you on huge legs as tall as redwood trees. Knowing you will be crushed if any part of this giant creature comes down on you, the three of you huddle like frightened mice in a clump of underbrush.

The huge dark shadow of the gigantic thing is hovering over your quivering bodies. You all three cover your mouths to keep from screaming, to keep from *breathing*.

For what seems like hours but is probably only a few seconds, the horrible giant stands still, listening. Then apparently giving up, it turns and wanders away.

*Turn to the next page.*

Cautiously the three of you stand up, look around, and continue down the trail.

After a while, Chris begins making stupid giant jokes. You are too tired to stop him, and besides, some of them are pretty funny. Darlene, though, has had enough of her brother.

"What do you get if you cross a giant's foot with a—?" he begins.

"Stop it!" she demands. "We nearly died . . . *again*. And all you do is joke around!"

You try to calm her, but she wants no part of you or Chris.

Mumbling something about finding civilization if it's the last thing she does, Darlene stomps away. You and Chris follow her a safe distance behind.

You tromp wearily along a rocky trail for what seems like hours when suddenly Darlene stops dead in her tracks. "There!" she shouts, pointing ahead. "Civilization, like I said!"

Down the trail in a drifting mist is a stairway. Made of stone, it seems to ascend into the sky.

"People had to have built those stairs!" she says, already bounding up them. "There's probably a gorgeous mansion at the top!"

She takes two and three steps at a time, running, clawing, stumbling happily upward, and you and

*Turn to the **next** page.*

Chris race after her, dreaming of civilization, of a warm bath, of a soft bed, of—

Suddenly you hear laughter. It is coming from below. You slacken your pace, stop, and look down. Your shock is twofold: the natives, no longer a single giant, are individuals again, but more frightening than that is the fact that all the stairs you have just climbed have vanished!

The natives, on solid ground a good thirty or forty feet below, are practically hysterical with laughter. One, as if making a joke for the benefit of others, pulls an arrow back in his bow, laughs, and lets it fly. It hits the stone lip of the stair at your feet, bounces off, and tumbles end over end back to the ground.

"Keep going!" you yell as the other natives laugh and shoot arrows. Each one hits a step disappearing right behind you, then sails back to earth.

You climb higher and higher, faster and faster, until you can no longer hear the natives laughing, and their arrows no longer even reach the vanishing stairs.

Gasping for breath, the three of you stop, and when you do the steps also stop disappearing. You gaze down. The natives are dot-sized, mere specks, hundreds of feet below.

"What do we do now?" asks Darlene.

You look from her to Chris. "There's nowhere to

*Turn to the next page.*

go but up." And with that you launch your exhausted body in motion—up the infinite set of stairs, as
your friends wearily follow.

"Look," Darlene says, pointing behind her. "The
stairs are disappearing again."

You and Chris don't even bother to look. You just
continue trudging forever upward.

On and on the three of you climb, until gradually you become aware that there seems to be a top to
the stairway. It is a haze of silver-gray blending to a
thick, creamy white. With little interest, too tired to
think, to really consider the possibilities, to worry, to
hold out any hope, you continue to climb.

As you approach closer to the haze, you realize it
is like a soft, spongy wall. It is very inviting . . . in a
comforting sort of way.

It is very close now. Not too many more steps.
And somehow, you know you will make it. You
assume Darlene and Chris are behind you, but you
are too tired to turn around and look back, to help
them, or even to encourage them on.

You count the steps ahead. Is it four or five? You
take one at a time. There is one more step, a last step
. . . and then . . .

"Ahh," you moan with contentment as the soft
whiteness envelops you.

*Turn to the next page.*

"Would you like another nice soft pillow?" Mrs. Muñoz asks, tucking a fluffy white down comforter around you. She climbs down the ladder attached to Chris's bunk bed. "I think I'll get you one." She turns back and smiles. "Chris told me you were having such a nightmare, and then, *for heaven's sake,* you started sleepwalking!"

You hear Chris laughing from the bed below you. You stare down the ladder at him, speechless with relief that your nightmare is over.

Though it is a bit farther away and will take longer to get to, you're sure the bony branch will make a better weapon. You dash to it, snatch it up, and charge at the spider. You stab its pulpy white back. It shrieks as yellow fluid spurts from the jagged hole.

Abandoning Chris and Darlene, the angry beast comes at you, clattering on its clawlike legs. Again you plunge in your spear—this time into its eye, and when you pull it out, white blood and clear fluid flow from the wound. The spider shudders, convulses, then finally goes limp.

You stumble to where Chris and Darlene lie motionless. They are scratched, bruised, and terrified, but they are OK. Darlene is sobbing. You put your arms around her, trying to calm her. You gently wipe the tears from her face.

"What are you doing?" she yelps.

Your eyes spring open. You are in the Muñoz home! Chris is asleep on the couch. You are in your sleeping bag, and Darlene is next to you, in hers. Your hand is on her face. She slaps it away. Groggily, half-asleep, she gazes at you.

"Huh?" is all you can manage to say.

"What are you doing, you idiot?" she groans.

"I . . . guess I . . . I was having a nightmare," you mutter.

*Turn to the next page.*

"You're weird," she mumbles, then rolls over and goes back to sleep.

You also try to go back to sleep, but are still shaken from your nightmare. You stare at the ceiling with eyes open wide. Finally they begin to droop, and as you drift back to sleep, you are unaware of a small spider silently gliding down from the ceiling on a thin silver strand.

Now in a very deep sleep, you are snoring. Will you wake up before the spider drops into your open mouth?

"Nah," you say, "I'm sure that old ship is interesting, but Darlene might be right. We'll probably drown trying to get to it, or worse, we might get eaten by sharks. Hey, that reminds me—I'm hungry."

"Me too!" say Darlene and Chris, almost in unison.

Together the three of you begin looking for something that might be edible. On the sand, rolling in and out on the lapping tide, is a small brown coconut. Darlene runs to it and snatches it up. She shakes it, and there is a sloshing inside. Getting down on her knees, Darlene smashes the coconut down on a rock, but nothing happens. "How come there's a coconut here but no trees?" she asks.

You shrug. "I guess it washed ashore from somewhere else."

Chris has now taken the coconut from Darlene and is beating it furiously against a rock. Hardly putting a dent in the thing, he tosses it in the sand at your feet. "You take a shot at it if you want, but personally, I don't think it's worth the effort."

*If you try to open the coconut,*
*turn to the **next page**.*

*If you don't bother with it,*
*turn to **page 105**.*

You flex your muscles like a bodybuilder. "Here," you say in a deep voice. "Let me give it a try."

Chris and Darlene laugh at you as you place the coconut on a cradle of coral and with all your might smash a heavy rock down on the thing. It cracks only slightly, so you hit it again, widening the crack. Then, with your fingers, you pry the hard shell apart.

To your amazement—and disgust—out slithers a large blue eyeball.

"Don't touch it!" warns Darlene.

But it is already too late. You have picked up the eye, and immediately you feel a terrible burning sensation in the palm of your hand. You try to pull the thing off, but you cannot get rid of it. Sticky and slimy, it is boring right into your hand as you fall to your knees in wretched pain.

Scared and horrified, Chris and Darlene back away, not knowing how to help you.

Meanwhile pain is shooting from your hand, up your arm, up the back of your neck, into your head. You stare at your hand and at the large blue eye embedded in your palm. Not only is it staring back at you, but you can see your own face by looking at yourself with your hand.

"Get rid of it!" yells Darlene. "Tear it off!"

The eye swivels and looks angrily at Darlene.

*Turn to the next page.*

You can see her with your own two eyes, and you can also see her with the eye in your hand. Then you look at Chris, scrounging around in debris. He picks up a stick with a pointed end. "I'll stab it with this!" he yells, aiming it at your palm.

The eye in your hand is staring at Chris with burning hatred. Electricity sparkles out from it, enshrouding Chris in a glittering white brilliance. He screeches in pain, runs in circles, and flails his arms at the electrical field buzzing around him.

You try to move your hand, to bury it in sand or to simply close your fist over the eye—anything to blind the thing and to stop it from what it is doing to Chris. But you can do nothing. Your hand is now completely controlled by the eye.

The sparkling shroud of electricity around Chris is now all but gone, and he is standing motionless. Slowly his skin turns gritty and rough all over, and he transforms into a sandstone statue.

Darlene rushes to him. As she touches his arm, he shrieks. His arm is soft and crumbly. It breaks off and falls to the sand.

She turns to you, terror on her face. "What did that horrible eye do to my brother?" she cries.

You cannot answer. Your hand, against your will, opens wide in front of Darlene's face. As though it

*Turn to the next page.*

were a television camera, you watch Darlene *through* your hand.

Suddenly a bolt of electricity shoots out from your hand right at her. Immediately her skin changes in the same way Chris's did, and then she, too, becomes a statue of sand . . . and topples over, right into her brother.

Chris's legs shatter at the knees; Darlene's head snaps off and rolls away down the beach. Right there on the sand, the mouth on her disembodied head cries out in pain.

You are overcome with grief and guilt. Then against your will, your hand turns over and you are forced to look at the hideous thing still stuck in your palm. The eye looks back at you. Electricity flares out from it, and watching yourself with the eye in your hand, you see your skin turn gritty and rough as you, too, slowly harden forever into a statue of sand.

"Maybe you're right," you tell Chris, turning away from the coconut. "Let's go see if there's something more edible on this island."

But after hours of trudging around, all you find is a mysterious-looking, octagonal-shaped box. It is very heavy, and has some kind of dial on top.

"Look at this," says Darlene, pointing to markings on the ancient-looking box that seem to indicate that the dial can be turned left toward a crosslike design, or right to a horizontal slash. The designs remind you of the negative and positive markings on a car battery.

"I guess we can turn the dial one way or the other," says Chris. "We have two choices."

"Actually," you correct him, "we have *three* choices. We can turn the dial left or right, or we can just forget about the box and not turn the dial at all."

*If you turn the dial to the left, toward
the cross, turn to the next page.*

*If you turn it right, to the horizontal slash,
turn to page 109.*

*If you decide not to turn the dial,
turn to page 120.*

You put your hand on the dial. "Well," you tell your friends, "guess I'll turn it to the left and see what happens." And with that, you turn it.

Suddenly you find yourself sitting on your bed in your own upstairs bedroom. You look around for Chris and Darlene, and for the island, but everything and everyone is gone. You feel very strange and very confused.

The sound of voices—and of weeping—filters up to you from downstairs. Curious, you go to investigate.

In the living room are many of your friends and relatives. Among them are Chris and Darlene. You try to make your way to them, but the room is so packed with people you can't get through. You call their names, but the drone of people talking drowns out the sound of your voice.

Behind you is your aunt. She is talking to John Peterson, a neighbor from across the street.

"I just feel like my heart is going to break," says Aunt Helen.

"It seems so unreal," adds your neighbor. "Just last weekend we were sitting in my yard, listening to the baseball game on the radio together."

"Such a waste," says Aunt Helen, lowering her eyes and shaking her head.

Across the room, you spot your mother sitting in

*Turn to the next page.*

a chair, tears flowing freely down her cheeks. You make your way through the crowd to her.

"What happened, Mom?" you ask.

The babble of voices is so loud she doesn't hear you. She turns and looks up as Mrs. Muñoz, Chris's mom, comes over and puts a hand on her shoulder.

"It hurts so bad," says your mother.

"Of course it does," says Mrs. Muñoz compassionately. "But the pain will ease with time."

Your mother wipes away her tears and stares off into space. "How could it have happened?" asks your mom. "They found the body in Malaysia but have no idea of the cause of death."

Your heart sinks. Your mom is talking about your brother or your father. You open your mouth to say something, but before you can get a word out, your mother gets up from where she is sitting. Her best friend, Lisa Brown, has just arrived, and your mom goes over to greet her. The two women embrace.

You spot Darlene making her way across the room.

"Hey, Darlene," you call, striding after her. "Wait up!"

She turns and looks around with a puzzled expression on her face, then disappears into a room with muted lighting.

You follow her, then stop at the doorway. The

*Turn to the next page.*

darkened room is filled with the color and fragrance of flowers, and in the center of it Darlene stands silently before a polished wood casket.

"You were really a special person," she whispers. "I'll miss you." Slowly she turns. Her face an expressionless mask, she walks from the room.

"Darlene," you say softly.

But Darlene doesn't answer. She glances in your direction. Then sobbing, unable to speak, she hurries away.

You turn and look back into the parlor, your eyes riveted on the casket. Who died? you ask yourself. The answer to the question is one you both do and do not want to know.

Tense, on stiff legs, you walk to the casket. An ungodly fear sweeps through you as you look down.

Your mouth opens in a scream as you see that the person in the casket is you.

"Let's try turning it right," you say, pushing the dial toward the horizontal line.

The instant you do this, you hear a terrifying sucking noise, and looking over your shoulder you stare in amazement at the ocean. It is parting in a great V-shaped wedge that extends far beyond the range of your vision. From somewhere deep in this canyon comes an odd moaning sound . . . a soft, enthralling chant.

Making your way down the beach, the three of you stand in awe of this vast canyon with walls of water. It looks so intriguing, so tempting, and the chanting voices seem to be calling you to come. You would like to enter this watery canyon—and feel a strong urge to do so—but obviously it could be very dangerous.

"Let's go in there," says Darlene eagerly.

"Looks pretty frightening to me," says Chris. He turns to you. "But it also looks really interesting. "What do you want to do? You want to go for it?"

*If you decide to enter the canyon of water,*
*turn to the next page.*

*If you decide not to enter it,*
*turn to page 115.*

"Yeah," you say, "let's check it out."

The three of you head down the seemingly endless canyon. As you walk along the ocean floor, you are fascinated by all you see. On the wet sand there is trash: bottles, cans, bits of paper, rusted pieces of metal—everything imaginable. There are lots of bones, too, *hundreds* of them—fish bones, animal bones, even human skulls.

As you carefully pick your way along, you pass through the rotted wood framework of what appears to be a sailing vessel that sank centuries ago.

Most fantastic of all are the twin walls of water on either side of you. The farther you go, the higher they become. Already they tower hundreds of feet above your head. And if you stop and look long enough, you can see fish and other marine life swimming deep within the dark, blue-green walls of water.

First an octopus glides past, followed by a school of silver-colored fish that zip into sight and then out. Finally a large bass comes up to the side, and as though behind glass in a huge aquarium, it gazes stupidly at you, its mouth slowly opening and closing.

Far ahead is a city of some sort. All the buildings are white, and they appear to be ancient.

As you approach the city, your pace begins to slow. The strange white buildings look eerie and ominous.

*Turn to the next page.*

Suddenly a moaning starts up. It seems to be emanating from the city.

"Maybe this is the lost city of Atlantis," says Darlene. "Anything's possible in this bizarre dream."

"Or maybe," you say, "it's the Valley of the Screaming Statues."

Chris looks up at the towering, V-shaped walls of water. "Well, it's not like any valley I've ever imagined, but even if the sides are of seawater, I suppose it's still a valley."

Entering the city, you are reminded of pictures you've seen of the ancient cities of Greece and Rome. The walls are of white alabaster, and the ceilings are supported by tall, beautiful columns of white stone. There are benches, walkways, pillars, and patios of the same stone. But it is not the objects that intrigue you the most—it is the people. They, too, are solid stone. And there are more and more of them the deeper you go into the city.

Everywhere stone people stand like statues; others lie on beds of stone, sit on chairs of stone, or lean against white, rock-hard trees. The stone people's mouths are fixed in wide-open gapes, and it seems that it is from the statues that the strange moaning hum is coming. Little by little, decibel by decibel, the volume and pitch of the sound increases.

*Turn to the next page.*

"Hey, where are you guys?" you hear Darlene call.

The three of you have been so enthralled by everything that you have wandered apart. Darlene calls again, and then you hear Chris's voice. You make your way down a stone passageway into a stone house.

You stop dead in your tracks. Darlene and Chris, with worried, sympathetic expressions on their faces, keep looking from you to a skeleton lying on the floor. Approaching them and kneeling down to take a closer look, you lift a bony wrist. On it is something very familiar. It is a watch—the expensive platinum and gold Omni Explorer 5000 that your father received as a gift from your mom on his fortieth birthday. Though corroded and waterlogged, there is no mistaking it; on the back there is an inscription: *Forty and Still Going Strong!*

"I think I've found my dad," you say sadly to Chris and Darlene, gently taking the watch from your father's wrist and slipping it onto your own. "I guess he followed the same route we did and this is where he ended up. He found it—the Valley of the Screaming Statues—and now so have we."

"It's so sad," says Darlene.

"In a way it's not," you say. "I haven't had my dad around for seven years. I knew deep down he was dead, and at least now I know what happened to him.

*Turn to the next page.*

But I wonder about my brother. I wonder if—"

Suddenly the ever-present sound of voices is terribly loud. It is a chorus of screams—a high-pitched, sirenlike warning!

Rushing from the house, you find the stone streets flooding with water. And miles in the distance, you can see the ocean collapsing, caving in upon itself, erasing the canyon as a horrifying mountain of water surges toward you.

"What do we do?" Chris and Darlene screech.

But you say nothing. There is nowhere to run, nowhere to hide. Nothing you can do.

Resigned to your fate, you watch as the sea approaches, its twin walls coming together, rushing toward you in a thundering, world-drowning roar.

There is not enough time to get a weapon. You lash out with your bare hands as the huge spider closes eight semi-transparent, sharp-pointed claws at you. You battle wildly, frantically, overcome with pain as the needlelike claws puncture your flesh. Horrified you see that it is injecting tiny, dot-size spiders into you. You scream.

And wake up in your sleeping bag in the Muñoz's home. You are bathed in sweat and terrified by your dream. But you are relieved that it is over . . . and that it was only a dream.

Chris is snoring away on the couch. You have to step over Darlene sprawled in her red sleeping bag as you make your way through the early morning gloom of the house. In the bathroom, you grab a towel to wipe the sweat from your forehead. But why do you feel so itchy? Flipping on the light and looking at yourself in the mirror, you go numb with horror. You see that your skin is moving, as if something is beneath the surface. Horrified, you are sure you know what it is . . . thousands of tiny, dot-sized spiders!

For a long while you study the seemingly end-less, boulevard-wide parting of the sea. "It's too dangerous," you finally say. "The sea might—"

"Oh, come on," says Chris, cutting you short. "Let's go in at least a little way. I mean, how often do you get to do something as weird as this?"

"Yeah," says Darlene.

You shake your head. "Sorry, guys. I'm not budging."

"Well, I guess it's just us," Chris says to Darlene, as they walk down the beach and into the water-walled trough.

"Good luck!" you yell, worried about your friends and feeling a bit like a coward.

As Chris and Darlene walk farther and farther out into the canyon, you sit down on the sand. You can hear them laughing, and you see them playing around. Every once in a while one of them stops to pick up something on the exposed ocean floor.

Your curiosity mounting, you are beginning to regret your decision to stay behind. Chris and Darlene are having such a great time, while you are just sitting on the beach, doing nothing at all.

Chris and Darlene are now pretty far away, perhaps a quarter of a mile down into the canyon. The slope is pretty steep. If they go much farther they'll

*Turn to the next page.*

soon be completely out of sight.

"Hey, you guys!" you call at the top of your lungs. "You're going too far. Head back *now.*"

Either they can't hear you or they're ignoring you. Regardless, they don't answer.

"You've gone far enough!" you try again.

Then you sit down. You feel like a party pooper, nagging at your friends and spoiling their fun.

Suddenly your eyes open wide. You are on your feet, staring in horror. The canyon of water is closing back up. You see Chris and Darlene running, and you hear them screaming in horror.

There is no hope for them.

In slow motion you see the rift in the ocean close, as miles-long twin avalanches of water slap together, collapsing and exploding upward in mountainous plumes of foam and spray. A giant wave roars against the shore and recedes. The sea, though still frothy, churning, and restless, returns to a state of relative normalcy.

Frantic, you run into the surf looking for your friends, praying that somehow by some miracle they survived. You see a bit of driftwood, and odds and ends of things churned up by the sea. But there is no sign of Chris or Darlene.

Dejected, you slog back onto the shore. Your sop-

*Turn to the next page.*

ping wet tennis shoes take on a layer of sand, making them look as though they're made of sandpaper.

You climb the knoll and turn and look out to the sea. All is gentle now, and calm, as though nothing had happened, as though Chris and Darlene had never existed.

Sending chills up your spine, you suddenly hear someone calling your name . . . from far, very far away. Could it be them? Did they get washed to shore? You look around, but there is no sign of them.

A hand taps you on the shoulder, and again your name is called—closer now—right in your ear.

And then your eyes open.

You are lying on your sleeping bag in the Muñoz home. It is morning. Somewhere in another room Mrs. Muñoz is talking excitedly on the telephone. Mr. Muñoz is standing over you, looking down at you.

He is usually a happy, good-natured man. But the expression on his face is now one of deep distress and worry.

"You slept here last night?" he asks.

"Yes, sir."

"In the living room?"

"Yes."

"And nothing happened—nothing unusual?"

You think for a minute. "No, sir, nothing—except

*Turn to the next page.*

I had a bad dream. But that's nothing. Is anything wrong, Mr. Muñoz?"

"Chris and Darlene—they're both missing," Mr. Muñoz says sadly.

"I've called everybody," says Mrs. Muñoz, entering the room, "and the police said they can't do anything until tomorrow." She begins to cry. "There's no trace of them—*anywhere!*"

You try to think of a logical explanation. But nothing comes to mind . . . except your nightmare. In bits and pieces, it comes back to you, especially the part where Chris and Darlene were swallowed up by the ocean.

But that was just a dream.

"I'm sure they're around somewhere," you tell Mr. Muñoz. "Maybe they got up early and—"

You stop what you are saying as you crawl out of your sleeping bag. Dread courses through every inch of your body. You are looking at your pants legs and your tennis shoes. They are wet and caked with sand.

The phone rings, and Mrs. Muñoz snatches it up. Her brow furrows as she listens. Suddenly she screams and, dropping the phone, walks woodenly toward you and Mr. Muñoz.

"What?" says Mr. Muñoz, fear in his eyes. "Who was that? What did they say?"

*Turn to the next page.*

Tears roll down her cheeks as she struggles to speak. "It was the Coast Guard. On an island, a hundred miles from here, they—they found two bodies." She bursts into anguished sobs. "They're of a boy and a girl who they think might be Chris and Darlene. They want us to come down and identify—" Now hysterical, Mrs. Muñoz can no longer go on.

"But that's not possible!" Mr. Muñoz cries.

Numb with horror, you sink down on the sofa. Your chin quivering, your eyes brimming with tears, you gaze at him, trying to find the words to tell him he is wrong.

Something bothers you about this strange, ancient box.

"We have no idea of what this thing is, where it came from, or what it will do," you tell your friends. "For all we know, it could be some kind of bomb. I'm not turning that dial either left or right. I'm just going to rebury this thing."

"Aren't you curious about what—if anything—it will do?" Darlene asks.

"I'm *very* curious. But I have a bad feeling about it—and we're not going to mess with it. *Comprendes?*"

She makes a face as you bury it, but says nothing.

"Hey!" calls Chris. He has wandered off a bit, and from a jumble of driftwood he's pulled several lengths of bamboo. "Let's make spears and go spear-fishing."

"Sounds cool," you say.

Darlene is also excited about the idea. Each of you takes up a length of bamboo, and using bits of metal, rock, and wood—any sharp objects you can find—fashion points for your spears.

Preparing to hit the water, Chris removes his glasses and places them carefully on a rock ledge. "I'll lead the way," he says.

You and Darlene both laugh at Chris. "*You?* How?" Darlene asks. "You can't see five feet in front of your face without your glasses."

*Turn to the next page.*

Chris chuckles. "Actually, I can barely see *one* foot in front of me without my glasses."

"Come on, old buddy." You take Chris by the elbow. "I'll be your seeing-eye dog."

Armed with your crude spears, the three of you wade into the warm, translucent blue water. Chris surface-dives, and you and Darlene follow suit. Though underwater, you can see as clearly as though on land. There are fish everywhere, in every size, shape, and color imaginable. You are fascinated, enjoying yourself immensely in this underwater world.

Your friends seem to be having a great time, too. Chris flashes past, squinting, in pursuit of a fish almost as big as he is. You catch a glimpse of Darlene below, swimming above what appears to be a crevasse or valley in the ocean floor. She seems to have spotted something down there.

Blowing bubbles and looking frightened, she rises to the surface, spits water, and pants for air. "Follow me!" she says. "It's strange . . . and horrible."

You surface-dive, follow her down, and enter an underwater valley. It is littered with corpses. They lie in piles, twisted together. A few are still standing.

You breaststroke close to one, then to others, and notice that none have eyes, and their flesh is hard to the touch. They look—and feel—like statues. Hair the

*Turn to the next page.*

texture of white needles sprouts out from some of the statues' heads. You touch one of the corpselike beings. It begins to moan, as do all the others. The moans rise in pitch, becoming a chorus of screams. Are they cries for help? Or appeals for you to join them?

You go up for air. "It's the Valley of the Screaming Statues!" you yell to Chris and Darlene.

You and your friends go down again—and again—looking for your brother and your father. You swim all through the valley examining every statue, but there is no trace of them.

Suddenly the harmonious wailing stops, and as it does, a milky white liquid begins to secrete from the pores of the ghastly underwater statues. The white liquid is rising, like a cloud of milk. You breaststroke frantically, trying to get away from it.

Finally reaching the surface, you breathe in huge lungfuls of air. Soon Chris's head bobs up, followed by Darlene's.

"That stuff is coming out of those . . . those people!" yells Darlene. "We've got to get away from it before it turns *us* into statues!"

"What are you guys talking about?" asks Chris, a helpless tone to his voice. "I saw the statues, but what do you mean by the stuff coming out of them? I didn't see anything."

*Turn to the next page.*

Knowing that Chris is nearly blind without his glasses, you quickly try to describe the frightening white liquid, but you are interrupted by a cry of terror from Darlene. Panic on her face, she is pointing in the direction of the island.

You stare in shock and disbelief. The island you left only minutes before is no longer there! Where once there was land is now only water.

The milky stuff continues to grow, continues to come at you. Together the three of you begin to swim as fast as you can. But the white splotch across the surface of the sea is about to overtake you.

Like a half-dead fish, you swim on. Your once strong, fast-paced strokes are now sloppy, lifeless flappings at the water.

"Chris!" Darlene suddenly yells.

You turn, then stare in horror. Chris is swimming right into the whiteness!

"Chris!" you shout. "You're going the wrong way!"

But your warning is too late. Already he is screaming in pain, thrashing in the midst of the white liquid and turning the color of alabaster. Adding to the horror, Darlene is swimming to her brother. She grabs hold of his hand of white stone—as she, too, changes. Together your two companions, transformed into statues, sink like stones . . . deep into the water.

*Turn to the next page.*

The murky whiteness continues to approach you. You are so tired, and so devastated by the loss of your friends, you consider letting it take you. But some last reserve of energy, some last desperate hope from deep within, causes you to begin swimming again.

You stop and tread water for a moment, trying to gather your strength, and something bumps into the back of your head. You turn and see a yellow rubber life raft behind you. In it, with his back to you, is a ragged, sick-looking man holding a paddle.

You grab hold of the soft rubber sides of the raft and hoist yourself aboard. "Where did you come from?" you ask.

The man turns around.

You gasp in horror. It is your father. But his flesh is rotted, and most of his hair has fallen from his head. He smiles at you, revealing black, decayed teeth, then turns again and begins paddling.

You lie in the bottom of the raft, totally exhausted, mourning the loss of your friends, filled with dread of your own father, a living corpse seemingly destined to forever travel the boundless sea.

Not understanding what is going on, not really even caring anymore, you close your eyes and drift on the edge of sleep. Beneath you, through the raft, you feel the gentle roll of the sea. It is soothing, comforting.

*Turn to the next page.*

You feel as though you could sleep forever.

"Wake up!" you hear someone say. And then you feel bouncing and rocking beneath you. It is a sickening, unpleasant feeling.

You open your eyes and find yourself on Chris's waterbed. He is laughing, pushing down on the bed, making the water slop around, rise and fall.

Darlene peeks her head in. "Breakfast is almost ready," she says, then hurries off downstairs.

"How did I get here?" you ask Chris.

"Don't you remember? You conked out in front of the TV. My mom told you to sleep in my room, and me—I got stuck with the couch."

Chris is studying you. "Are you OK? You look like you've seen a ghost. You're as white as chalk."

"No, I just had a bunch of weird nightmares. All kinds of 'em, all connected together."

You start to tell him about your dreams, but he seems uninterested. Paying no attention to you, he turns and walks out of the room.

Wondering at his behavior and a bit annoyed by it, you make your way into the bathroom and splash cold water on your face. Drying off, you return to the bedroom . . . and suddenly go rigid with fear.

Sitting in a chair at the window, his back to you, is a ragged, bone-thin man.

*Turn to the **next page**.*

"Who are you?" you cry, afraid of the answer.

The man turns around.

You gasp in horror. It is your father. But his flesh is rotted and only a few strands of hair still sprout from his wrinkled scalp. He smiles at you, revealing black, decayed teeth.

"Are you awake?" he asks.

"I—I think so," you stammer.

"Or are you still asleep," he continues, "imagining you are awake?"

"I don't know," you tell him, totally bewildered.

"There's no way you *could* know," your father says, resting his decayed head on a finger of bone. "And it doesn't really matter, does it?"

"What do you mean?"

"Either way—awake or asleep—your nightmare never ends."

Just
when you
thought
it was safe
to fall
asleep . . .

... Watch out
for these
other

---

# NIGHTMARES!
## HOW WILL YOURS END?

---

titles:

CASTLE OF HORROR

CAVE OF FEAR

PLANET OF TERROR